MUCUS
MAYHEM

Kevin Sylvester

Illustrations by Britt Wilson

Scholastic Canada Ltd.
Toronto New York London Auckland Sydney
Mexico City New Delhi Hong Kong Buenos Aires

To my kid Baz, who has helped me research this book
for years! Achoo! And their sibster, Erin, who has
helped us pick the most equitable tissues.
— K.S.

Scholastic Canada Ltd.
604 King Street West, Toronto, Ontario M5V 1E1, Canada

Scholastic Inc.
557 Broadway, New York, NY 10012, USA

Scholastic Australia Pty Limited
PO Box 579, Gosford, NSW 2250, Australia

Scholastic New Zealand Limited
Private Bag 94407, Botany, Manukau 2163, New Zealand

Scholastic Children's Books
Euston House, 24 Eversholt Street, London NW1 1DB, UK

www.scholastic.ca

Library and Archives Canada Cataloguing in Publication
Sylvester, Kevin, author
        Mucus mayhem / Kevin Sylvester ; illustrated by Britt Wilson.

(The almost epic squad)
Issued in print and electronic formats.
ISBN 978-1-4431-5779-7 (hardcover).--ISBN 978-1-4431-5780-3 (ebook)

        I. Wilson, Britt, 1986-, illustrator II. Title.

PS8637.Y42M83 2018   jC813'.6   C2018-901939-5
                                                C2018-901940-9

Illustrations and hand lettering by Britt Wilson.
Cover background image © Piotrurakau/Getty Images.

6 5 4 3 2 1   Printed in Canada 114   18 19 20 21 22 23

3

7

CHAPTER 1

THIRTEEN YEARS LATER

The Gorg threw its flaming axe. I ducked, the twirling inferno singeing the ends of my long amber braids. I fell to one knee, head snapping back up, ready, watching.

The lips of my mortal enemy curled into an evil smile, his slime-covered fangs grinding horribly. "This ends now, Fairfax the Elfling." He reached for a sword from his pack, igniting it with a nostril snort.

I moved my right hand behind my back, concealing it. *Time to wipe that grin off your ugly mug,* I thought. Then I yelled, "Come get me, butt for brains!"

The Gorg charged. I mouthed the words to the armour charm and watched as a titanium glove cloaked my right hand. With a horrible shriek, the

Gorg threw the sword. I leaped and snatched it out of mid-air, the metal making a loud *thunk* as it smacked against my hand.

"Ha!" I said, closing my fist and crumbling the sword like a pop can. My body glowed an eerie green as its energy flowed through me. I raised my eyes to the Gorg and smiled. His grin evaporated, replaced by a look of utter horror. He turned to run.

"Why the hurry? Got a date?" I curled into a ball and rolled forward, picking up speed. In one smooth motion I landed at the Gorg's feet, unfurled, unsheathed my own sabre, and cut through the muscular back of the beast. He howled in rage and pain and exploded in a gush of blue flame. Gobs of slime flew into the air, then rained down on the ground.

Where the Gorg had stood was now a smouldering hole. Out of the ashes rose the words I had been hoping for, emblazoned on two gold coins: *1,000 Points, 1 Life.* I grabbed the coins, the air chiming with music. Not just music — the electronic sound of VICTORY!

There was a *beep* and a message from beancounter3000x appeared at my feet: "Nice one, Fartface. Next time it's my turn."

"You wish," I typed. "And the name is Fairfax."

But beancounter3000x had logged off, their real identity still a mystery. He or she kept showing up to attack me whenever I got close to a castle or stash of weapons or power bars. Of course, I always won. But he or she was a pain.

I sheathed my sabre and looked for the floating arrows that would tell me where I needed to go next. I was already a Seventh-Level Warrior. Two more Life Tokens and I'd be a Grand Master, just like my mom before me. "May the Council of Greats allow her an eternity in the heavens," I said, bowing my head in her memory. But before I could move another muscle, a loud voice boomed in my ears.

"Jess! Dinnertime! Pause that silly game and get up here." It was my mom, my real mom, very much alive, calling down the basement stairs.

Dinnertime? I looked at the wall clock. Breakfast was a distant memory. Lunch? Apparently never happened. I shook my head. I'd been playing for eight hours? I let my controller hover over the "Quit Game and Save?" icon, a tremor of regret momentarily fighting with my need for food. I clicked.

My avatar gave a short wave and the screen went dark. I could see my reflection. The real me. No long, elegant braids or awesomely ripped muscles. Just messy dark hair, a face that was starting to break out and a nose that glowed like Rudolph's. Ugh.

"Jessica *Flem*!" Uh-oh. Full name and angry-mom

voice. "Dinner is getting cold and I cooked your favourite, rigatoni!"

"You cooked OUR CAT?" I yelled.

Yes, I named our cat RigaTony. He replaced our old cat, RigaMortis, who, sadly, lived up to her name after a run-in with a snowplow. I cocked my ear, waiting to see how Mom would take the joke.

"Ha, ha," she said, her voice softer. "Now, c'mon."

"Whew." I breathed a sigh of relief. Still. Time to move, which wasn't as easy as I'd hoped. My butt was seriously asleep and I knew from experience that the more it woke up, the more it would feel like my undies were filled with stinging ants. I got up, slowly.

Suddenly a shadow flew at me from the computer. Something landed on my head. Sharp talons dug into my scalp. "AHHHHHHHHHH," I shrieked. The shadow answered with a howl and a hiss. My controller flew through the air, breaking a nearby lamp. The shadow jumped in alarm, its paws flailing in the air.

"RigaTony!" I yelled. And then it started: full-blown booger barrage, running nose, jammed lungs.

"Puffer, where's my puffer?" I croaked, hyperventilating. See, I'm allergic to cats, among about a million other things, and the basement is supposed to be a cat-free zone.

RigaTony must have snuck down when Mom opened the door to call me for dinner. I reached around on the floor in a panic, gasping for air. He licked his paws and stared at me. Was he smiling?

"You demented dust bunny," I croaked. He coughed up a furball, right in my face! My nose began to jam up like a blocked toilet. Puffer not found; tissues now the priority. I lunged for the nearest box — there were always ten or so close by — and blew. A tiny bit of relief as oxygen, for one split second, was able to pass through my nose.

I threw the tissue at RigaTony, who hightailed it back up the stairs like he'd been shot. That was weird. Why was a cat so afraid of a snotty tissue?

I looked around at the mess. In *Gang of Greats*, messes magically disappeared. The lamp did not appear ready to co-operate. It was a lamp my dad had made from an old bottle of some disgusting drink called Splotnik. *Splotnik. Proudly bottled in Dimly* was written in a kind of neon-orange paint on the glass. Well, now it was more like *Splo, Pro, Dim* and *ik* on a bunch of glass fragments.

"I wish I had someone to clean this up," I said out loud. Maybe Mom would hear me and decide this was a good birthday present. Fairfax was 125, pretty young for an elf. I was about to turn thirteen.

No response from Mom, other than the tapping of her foot on the kitchen floor, clearly waiting for me to emerge from my *crypt*, as she calls it. I turned to follow the cat up to the kitchen. But as the stairway light went out, I caught a glimpse of something moving on the floor behind me. Rats? Mice? I turned the light back on and stared. Had a tissue moved? I glared at it. It glared back. As motionless as, well, a tissue.

"Dinner! Now or never!" Mom yelled, her voice back to 8.5 on the grumpy setting.

I shook my head and turned off the light.

CHAPTER 2

ACHOO!

There are many weird things about my life. Top among them? My parents. I'm asthmatic. So, of course, Mom and Dad are cat people. They adopt stray cats, rescue cats, *fluffy* cats. RigaMortis almost did me in. She certainly almost cleaned out my parents' bank accounts, thanks to the massive tissue sales. Of course, every time I sneeze or hack up my own version of a hairball, Mom says, "Don't worry, Jess. Most kids grow out of their childhood allergies."

Mom! I'm turning *thirteen*. Not going to happen! Jeepers. And I'm allergic to just about every plant under the sun. So, what does Mom do for a living? She's a *florist*. Our house is always filled with new species of some "aromatic" lilac or day lily.

On the flip side, Dad is an accountant, so I'm only allergic to his boring conversations about tax codes and monetized investment strategy and . . . ugh.

I believe I'm allergic to the sun too, although Mom says it's because I spend all my time inside playing video games. Why wouldn't I, when every living thing *outside* wants to kill me? The kids at school think I'm some kind of goth because I'm always wearing long, dark hoodies and jeans, even in Dimly's three hours of actual summer. So that hasn't exactly made me "popular."

Oh, and there's also the story about my birth. Apparently I had great lungs and, as my dad puts it, a nose as clear as the sky on a winter morning. He says I cried like a foghorn for hours after I was born. Then, all of a sudden, one night my whole pulmonary system went *kablooey*. The doctor, Dr. Fassbinder, said he had no idea exactly what happened. And my parents couldn't ask the nurse who was on duty because she died in some bizarro accident. Like, she blew up or something. Mom is a little vague on the details.

But as weird as all that is, the weirdest thing happened this morning. I woke up early and went downstairs to get in some G of G practice. The big tournament is just a couple of weeks away. Online. Head-to-head. Worldwide. Win until you lose. Two years ago, I was the best player from Dimly. Okay, there were only two of us, and that geeky kid from school, Gary Lundborg, barely made it out of his first game. Last year I was top ten in North America. This year I'm going for the whole enchilada. GLOBAL DOMINATION!

Anyway, I opened the basement door. A quick scan showed that RigaTony was off doing something upstairs. Probably peeing on my homework. So I flicked on the light and made a beeline for my computer. I hit the last step and stopped cold. The whole basement was — get this — clean.

No, not just clean. *Spotless.*

The lamp had been tossed out. The pieces? Gone. The tissues? Disappeared. The empty chip bags? Vanished. The socks, underwear, T-shirts? Departed! And that petrified stuff that might once have been french fries? Okay, I don't know any more words for gone. It was all gone!

My controller was sitting on the for-the-first-time-ever-visible coffee table. The top was glass? Who knew? The couch cushions were fluffed — *fluffed!* — and in the right place. The hypoallergenic bamboo floor had even been scrubbed and dusted.

I sniffed and actual air passed through my nose, which, for once, did not automatically get jammed with snot. No cat hair! I breathed through my nose again and smiled. Mom and Dad must have cleaned my crypt while I was sleeping!

"Fourth-best birthday present ever," I said, laughing. Of course, I wasn't giving up hope for the phone I wanted. That way I could play G of G when I was at school. The mobile version, at least. Not the same as the online game, but a good way to practise.

I settled into my favourite spot on the couch, without the usual sound of potato chips being crunched under my butt, and flicked on my game. A message immediately shot up on the Start screen from

AsseomeDud27. Gary Lundborg's gamer name. He told me he'd been trying to type "AwesomeDude27," but apparently hit the wrong keys with his huge thumbs and then *enter* by accident.

"Weirdest visit with dr F evr! We should talkl."

I checked the time. He'd sent it hours before, at way-too-early in the morning Montreal time. Every year we all have a checkup with Dr. Fassbinder, the guy who, as my mother likes to say OUT LOUD, *birthed* us. We being me, Gary and two other kids, Daisy and Archie. Or maybe it was Artie? Arnie? He moved away when he was just a kid. Daisy . . . sigh. She and I hung out all the time, until she moved away last year. We still write to each other but it isn't the same. Anyway, Gary must be asleep by now if he'd been up that early. I'd message him back later.

Fassbinder. Darn it. I'd hoped he was going to skip this year. Today wasn't just my birthday, it was also the day for my annual checkup. Usually the doc springs for a trip to Montreal for me and my family. Dad goes to some hockey thingy (*any* hockey thing: game, practice, puck factory) while Mom and I sit in Dr. Fassbinder's office at the — get this — *Boredom* Institute (or *Institut de l'ennui*) where I get prodded, probed and asked these useless questions about my nose, my allergies, my "sense of self-worth."

They sure got the name right. BOOOOOOORING. Then Dr. F. would start asking me these weird questions about whether I ever "found myself flying" or "moving things with my mind." So last year I switched up my answers a bit. Why? BECAUSE I WAS BORED. Mission accomplished.

"Have you ever shown any . . . magic powers?" he asked.

I made my eyes go as wide as they could and looked straight at him. "Yeah."

Mom gave a short growl. I ignored her. Dr. F. practically leaped on top of his desk, his ponytail swishing like RigaTony's tail. "Really?"

You should have seen his eyes bug out.

"Yeah. In *Gang of Greats*."

"Is that some kind of special group of kids?"

I nodded. "Oh yeah."

I think he began to drool. There was a weird squeaking noise from behind him as he chuckled loudly and happily.

"We might finally be getting somewhere!" he yelled over his shoulder.

More squeaking. It was kind of fun watching him go progressively nuts.

"Gary is in the gang too," I said.

"Gary Lundborg?!"

"Yup. He's a Troll."

"A . . . troll?" His elation wavered slightly, and his eyes narrowed. The air started coming out of him like the slow leak of a balloon.

"Yeah. I'm an Elfling. Sixth Level." I shrugged, like it was no big deal. "But I should be Seventh soon."

His face fell faster than the temperature in Dimly in February. "You're talking about a board game," he said.

"Board game? Do I look a hundred years old? I'm talking about *Gang of Greats*. It's, like, the best video game ever."

I've never seen Dr. F. mad — well, not angry-mad anyway — but I can now say I've seen him sad. He slunk back in his chair and covered his face with his right hand. He waved his left hand at me and Mom.

"Go," he said. "Happy birthday."

Mom was cheesed. She ushered me out of there so fast my head spun. "That was not funny, young lady," she said, as we sprinted through the waiting room. "Dr. Fassbinder helped deliver you."

"Don't you mean *birth* me?" I said.

"No more sass from you, Jessica Flem."

Mom had used my full name. She was definitely angry-mad.

But, you know what? I can do mad too. "Look. I answered BassFinder's questions. And I'm sick of being treated like some kind of freak. 'Have you ever found yourself flying?' Who does he think I am? A lab rat? I'm sick of these visits. Why do I have to do these? Every. Single. Year?"

Mom had just looked away. "It's complicated."

I waited, but that seemed to be all the explanation I was going to get. "I'm not stupid," I said. "Explain it to me."

"Some day." She got a faraway look in her eye. "I'm not even sure *I* know exactly what's going on." Finally she sighed and put a hand on my shoulder. "Let's go get your father."

So, bottom line, this year we struck a compromise. Dr. F. would still do the checkup, but online before school started. I expected it to take two minutes, tops. Then he'd be done with me, hopefully forever, and I could just get on with my life . . . or at least my G of G practice. (Which, TBH, is way more important.)

He wasn't supposed to check in for a few minutes, so I turned back to the game. But, just as I was about to start looking for more Life Tokens, the doorbell rang. I heard Mom or Dad shuffling, muffled voices, and then a familiar one, calling out.

"Jessiekins! Happy birthday, sweetie!"

Rats. Garvia Greep.

CHAPTER 3

GREEPED OUT

Garvia Greep has been my babysitter pretty much from the day I was born. Nurse Nussbaum — the one who my parents tell me was nice, and who also then inconveniently blew up — apparently assigned Greep to keep an eye on me as soon as I started coughing. Then Nussbaum croaks and, the way the Grim Greeper tells it, the contract never got cancelled. So she's kept an eye on me ever since. Both eyes, actually. All. The. Time.

When I was young she'd take care of me when my parents were at work, or sick. Normal, right? But then, even after I turned ten, she'd just keep showing up, helping around the house, putting me to bed and reading bedtime stories.

And no *Goodnight Moon* for me. She brought her own kids' books, like, written and illustrated *by* her. They were always about wicked witches or murderous beasts who were "misunderstood," even when they were eating kittens or rampaging through villages of cute bunnies. I'm not making that up. Scary books: *Goldilox and Bagels, Unicorn on the Cob.*

And then, when I'd wake up with the inevitable nightmare, she'd be watching me. Not checking on me to make sure I was okay either. It was as if she'd been waiting for me like the hungry wolf in her book *The Three Little Pigs in a Blanket.* One night I woke up and she was hovering over me with a stethoscope and a measuring tape.

Now, upstairs, she called again: "Jessiekins? Happy birthday! Where are you hiding, you little scamp?"

I tried to stay as still as possible. Maybe she'd think I was asleep. But no such luck. That woman was like a human bloodhound. "I have a present for you," she sang. "I just bet you are downstairs."

I turned up the volume on the game, just as a Battle Goat trampled onto the screen. Easy win. Five hundred points.

Suddenly, my nose began to run. What was her present? A down pillow? No. She was wearing some kind of pungent perfume, and as it wafted ahead of her down the stairs, it triggered all of my allergies. It was like roses, lilacs, rosemary and burnt rubber. She hadn't ever worn that before. Or had she but I'd never been able to smell it?

My head was swimming. But then my nose completely jammed and I began my tissue tango — nose, tissue, garbage basket. Or, more accurately, floor. Nose. Tissue. Floor. Repeat. Cha-cha-cha.

I felt her clammy hand on my shoulder. "Pause the game, sweetie. Let's talk!" Her voice sounded sickly sweet, like a snake trying to do a Taylor Swift imitation.

I paused the game and turned to look at her. Her face was so close I could feel her breath. That wolfy hunger was back in her eyes as they swept over me. "You look awake . . . I mean older!" she said. "Anything else . . . different?" She winked.

"Um . . . I let out a really good belch this morning. Spelled almost half the alphabet."

She stood up straight but kept the crocodile smile plastered on her face. "Still my funny little Jessiekins. Here." She handed me a wrapped package. It was obviously a book. Despite myself, I groaned, certain it was going to be a new copy of *Little Dead Riding Hood*. I hesitated over the pink wrapping paper, my least favourite colour.

"It's not one of *my* books," she said, guessing my

thoughts. "It's a diary. You know. Every teen girl needs one to chronicle her . . . changes."

"Changes?" I blurted, despite myself. *Idiot!* Free advice: never ask adults what they mean by stuff like that!

Luckily, Greep avoided the obvious and kept it vague. "It's a time of many . . . transformations and . . . developments." She began to raise her hands to demonstrate some example of what *that* meant.

"Okay. TMI," I said quickly. I noisily opened the present. The diary looked just like a diary. Flowers on the outside, of course, and about a hundred lined pages inside.

"Thanks," I said. "It's kind of heavy for a book, though, isn't it?"

She smiled. "Heavy-duty paper. Only the very best for my little Jessiekins." She handed me a fancy-looking pen — heavy, metal, with my name inscribed in silver along the side. "And this is for writing down your innermost thoughts and dreams . . . and plans."

"Wow," I said. It was actually pretty nice.

I was about to say thanks again, a new record for me and the Greeper, when my computer buzzed. I turned to look. It wasn't the game. There was a call coming through.

"It's Dr. Fassbinder," I said, turning back around. But Greep was rushing up the stairs, waving at me frantically. "I just remembered I have an appointment," she said. "Happy birthday!" Then she was gone.

The computer buzzed again. I answered and Fassbinder's face filled the screen. His chin rested on his hand. His eyes lazily searched me out on his own screen. He looked tired.

"Hello, Jess. Happy birthday." Then he began asking me the standard questions. How was I feeling, blah blah. I answered them as quickly as I could, between blowing my nose and tossing the tissues over my shoulder. A nice little pile was forming back there.

Then the weird questions started again.

"Any flying?"

"No."

"Any ability to move things with your mind?"

"No."

"Any super strength?"

"Seriously? I can barely walk up the stairs without losing my breath."

"I'll take that as a no." He sighed. Then he seemed to see the Mount Everest of tissues for the first time.

"Don't you have someone to clean up that stuff?"

"Like a home version of a school janitor?" I laughed. "I wish."

Then, bit by bit, Dr. F.'s eyes started to seriously bug out. "Is–is–is–is– that a–a–a–a– . . ." he spat out.

"Is what a what? You feeling okay, Doc?"

He seemed unable to answer. He pointed. Not at me, but behind me. Had Garvia come back? RigaTony? Then I heard a sound, like someone or some*thing* shuffling. I turned around slowly and froze.

The pile of tissues was moving. Like an iceberg on the ocean, the top of the pile seemed to float above the back of the couch. It reached the arm and turned. And just like an iceberg, there was a lot more than the tip. You see, the pile wasn't moving on its own.

There was a small man pushing it. He was wearing a janitor's uniform. But he, and the uniform, were sort of glossy green and see-through. Like a rancid gummy bear. He stopped, gave me a little salute, then resumed pushing Mount Snotrag past the TV and toward the wall.

"AH!" I jumped away so fast I fell on my controller. Fassbinder's face disappeared from the screen with a blip.

The janitor grew and grew as he came in contact with more of my, and I apologize for this image, nose-goo-packed tissues. Once he reached the far end of the room, he was almost as tall as me.

He grabbed a garbage bag from somewhere behind the TV and threw all the tissues inside. Then he looked around the room, which was spotless again.

He slapped his hands together in the universal sign for "job well done" and climbed into the bag. He was getting smaller but his arms, as they shrank, tied the bag closed. There was a gurgling noise and the bag went still.

There might have been other things going on around me, but I was oblivious. At some point I noticed my computer ringing and ringing. Dr. F. trying to reconnect. I wasn't ready to talk to him. Not yet.

I slipped off the couch and tiptoed over to the bag. I nudged it. Nothing moved, but the bag jiggled and sloshed, like if someone had spilled a jumbo root beer in the bottom. Gross. Where had that thing come from? I closed my eyes and tried to remember what had happened before the green man appeared. I'd been talking to Dr. F. He'd asked me if I had a cleaner. I'd said, "I wish." Then, boom. Some goopy green guy starts cleaning up the room.

No way. Was that what happened yesterday too? I quickly grabbed a tissue, blew my nose, and threw the tissue onto the floor. "I wish I had a janitor," I said. But the tissue just sat on the floor staring back at me, indifferent and unresponsive.

I tried a couple more times — I mean, I needed to blow my nose anyway — but still nothing. Dr. F. continued to ring and ring. I climbed back over to the couch and clicked on "Answer" and the screen came to life. A white mouse's head filled the screen. The mouse, and I swear this happened, turned around and said, "She's back," then disappeared. Dr. F.'s face reappeared with the biggest grin I've ever seen.

"Doc. What happened?"

"Jess. I think your mucus just cleaned your basement. I hoped this day would come."

There was a gasp from someone at the top of the basement stairs, then hurried footsteps on the floor above followed by the bang of the front door closing.

CHAPTER 4

HAPPY BIRTHDAY, SNOT-FACE!

So, you'd think something this revolutionary would have kept me home from school? Nope.

After I told Fassbinder I couldn't do the janitor trick again, his grin faded, a little. "Gary had some limitations too," he said, tapping a finger against his top lip.

A tiny voice from somewhere at his feet called out, "But Archie is amazing!"

Dr. F. smiled, a dreamy look in his eyes. "Yes. Such an incredible guy."

"Hey, Doc," I said, snapping my fingers. "Remember me? Jess?"

He shook his head. "Um. Sorry. Look. I'll talk to your parents later, but be very careful who you reveal this power to."

"Power? This is the most useless and disgusting superpower I could possibly imagine!"

"You do seem to have a clean basement there," he said.

I rubbed my eyes. He had a point. "Dr. F. What's going on?"

He looked at me with a kind smile. "Ah, Jess. It's a long story. Perhaps it's best if your parents tell you. They have a . . . secret dossier . . . that might help clear things up."

And then the screen went blank. That was it. All the explanation I was going to get. Being a kid sucks sometimes.

I sat there, dumbfounded. So much was happening and it was all confusing. I picked up the diary Greep had given me. I thought it might help to keep track of stuff that was going on. I do this with G of G sometimes, write down things that have worked in a battle, or spells that require a lot of numbers. Not that I thought I'd ever forget anything I'd just seen, but it never hurt to be prepared. I jotted down the events of the last few minutes, underlining the word "dossier?"

Mom was shuffling around in the kitchen, clanking a frying pan. I couldn't smell a thing but I was pretty sure she was making my traditional birthday pancakes. For once, I'd have them on my actual birthday in my actual home and not some deli near the stupid Boredom Institute. I closed the diary, reluctantly turned off the game, and went upstairs.

Talking to Mom turned out to be kinda useless. She was so busy fussing over the stove that she barely registered anything. It was like she was in a daze.

"Dr. F. says he's going to call you later."

"Um-hmm," she said, flipping the pancake and staring at it like RigaTony staring at a bright light.

"Greep leave?" I asked.

Mom seemed confused. "Garvia? Was she here?" She walked over, but only to put a vase of cut pink roses in front of me. "These are fresh," she said. "Just smell them."

"I assume that's a joke?" I said grumpily. Then I sneezed and blew my nose. Cha-cha-cha.

"Such pretty flowers," she said, flipping the pancake. It made a spitting sizzle in the pan.

"I heard you guys talking."

"I don't think you did, darling," she said, her voice a bland monotone, staring at the griddle.

"That's some fascinating pancake," I joked. She didn't respond. "Well. Maybe she was talking with Dad?"

"Your father is out. He's in line for tickets to the big outdoor hockey game."

"Oh." The game between the Winterpeg Gents and the Barfalo Slaybirds. I think I have the names right. Outdoors at Dimly Field. Two weeks from today. The biggest thing to happen to Dimly in, like, well, forever.

"So, I can apparently do this thing with my boogers," I said, trying the direct route.

"Jess. Language," she said.

Thanks for missing the point, Mom. Honestly. "But, I can *do* things. Like make a janitor to clean the basement."

"Yes, dear," she said. "That's nice. Now eat your breakfast. I've got to go to work."

And that was it. She walked out of the kitchen and straight outside. She wasn't even wearing a jacket. I jotted down in my diary, "Mom acting super weird."

The next thing I knew, she was starting the car. There's a joke my dad tells: How do you know when it's winter in Dimly? Answer: it's *always* winter in Dimly. So, in Dimly you never just get in a car and start driving. Unless you *like* frostbite. You need to warm up the seats and then go. I assumed she was just doing that before driving me to school. Standard practice.

I wolfed down the pancakes and sprinted to grab my school stuff. But just as I was tying up my boots, I heard her pull away. I ran outside, jacket unzipped, one bootlace slapping my ankles, my backpack sagging from one shoulder.

The car turned the corner and disappeared. The door closed behind me. Locked. I looked for my keys. Inside, of course. It started snowing. Great.

I zipped up my coat and trudged off to school.

I don't have a lot of friends. Okay. I have one. His name is Heathcliff Bell Snuffington . . . the Third. Stop laughing. His dad is some English aristocrat. Teaches stuff about languages, or maybe rocks, at Dimly University. So it's not Cliff's fault that he's got a name that makes him sound like somebody's demented teddy bear.

Anyway, that's what's left for available friends after your buddy Daisy goes off to the Wet Coast so her mom can "find herself" and all the cool kids have picked their "teams" at school. Snot-face and Heathcliff Bell Snuffington . . . the Third. The rejects.

So at first we kind of hung out by default. Then we started actually getting along. He makes me laugh. I get him into trouble he's too chicken to get into himself.

"Happy birthday, snot-face!" he called as I made my way up the school steps, snow falling off me like mini-avalanches.

"Ha, ha," I said. "I've had a bizarre morning, okay?" I'd run out of tissues about three seconds from my house and had wiped my nose on the back of my gloves so many times, they were as stiff as cardboard. I'd tried conjuring up something like a taxi driver or even a bike, but nothing.

Cliff opened the door for me. The warm air hit my face like a welcome summer breeze.

"So, what's the plan for the big day? Apart from annihilating a forest's worth of trees with your nose."

"About that," I said. "You'll never believe me when I tell you what happened." I told him everything.

"I don't believe you," he said.

"He got bigger! It was like he was absorbing more of my nose stuff through osmosis."

"I think you mean *snoz-mosis*. And I still don't believe you." I locked my eyes on his and gave him my best best-friend stare. It took only three seconds.

"You *are* serious!" he said, his jaw gaping. "You can actually make a snot golem!"

"Shhhh!" I said, noticing the looks we were getting from the other kids.

"He was just a janitor," I said in almost a whisper. "Not some dude from *The Hobbit*."

"No, no. Not Gollum. Golem. It's this hero-monster thing. Created out of mud, it comes to life by magic to help protect people at the time they need it the most. Dad teaches about stuff like that."

I thought back to my saluting, not-so-epic goober janitor. "Not sure he was protecting me," I said. "More like shoving old tissues in the garbage."

"Protecting you from germs, maybe?" Cliff offered.

I shrugged. "I can't seem to do it again."

"Not exactly Spider-Man or Captain America, are you?" he joked. "More like Booger-Girl."

"Grrr. I'll stick with Fairfax the Elfling," I said.

"Speaking of which, as it is your one hundred twenty-ninth birthday, I have a present." He held out a box of tissues with a red bow tied across it.

"One hundred twenty-sixth birthday," I said, grabbing one just as my nose defrosted and began running with renewed vigour.

"It's new," he said, pointing at the words *It's New*

on the box. "Lotion AND lip balm. Ten-ply industrial strength. TEN! Isn't modern science amazing?"

"Like blowing my nose on a cloud," I said, dropping the tissue in a garbage can.

He shuddered. "That is the most disgusting image you've ever given me. And . . ."

"Don't you dare."

". . . and images that vivid must be preserved." He pulled out his phone and walked over to the can.

"Cliff, no." People were staring again. I tried to hide my head in my hands, dreading what I knew was about to happen.

"Art thou not a lover of great art?" he said, feigning shock. He began snapping images of the used tissue. Then he carefully picked it up by a corner and put it in a plastic sandwich bag he'd grabbed from his pocket.

He walked back and held up the phone, sliding his thumb between snapshots of at least a hundred used tissues I'd tossed over the past year. Cliff thought it was hilarious. He called them my "ori-gummy" creations.

"Look, a boulder. Another boulder!" He kept swiping until he came to this morning's pic. "And this one does, in fact, look very much like a cumulonimbus."

"Please tell me you don't still have all those tissues in a box somewhere."

"On the contrary. I have each one labelled and

identified in a separate acid-free display bag. Dated and marked. They fill a bookshelf in my room. The archaeologists and museum curators of the future will thank me." It clearly wasn't just his name that got him stuck in the reject zone with me.

The bell rang for first period.

"Zombies move faster than a school kid in the morning," Cliff said.

"At least they aren't staring at us anymore."

"There's still the afternoon," Cliff said helpfully.

"Ugh."

Cliff and I got together again at lunch. Since Mom had neglected to make one before bailing on me, I had to mooch half of Cliff's anchovy and brie baguette. I was that hungry. It had the texture of a cookie someone had dropped in a toilet.

"How's the birthday so far?" he asked, watching me try not to gag.

"Most people just talked about the big hockey game, and how it is going to 'put Dimly back on the map.'"

Cliff nodded. "It's this new thing called SynthetICE. Made right here. If it works, people can play hockey outside all year round!"

"Yippee."

"C'mon. This is good news. We got a whole lecture about it in science class," Cliff said. "Dimly used to be a big manufacturing centre."

"Dimly Bulbs," I said. "Dad got his start as an accountant for them. There's still a crate of bulbs in the garage. He calls it his severance package."

"It was world famous. They made bulbs that were supposed to last a lifetime, using some weird thing called reidium."

"Reidium?" It sounded familiar but I wasn't sure why. I opened up my diary and made a note to check on it later.

"A rare element. Hard to find these days. There were all these experiments done with it way back when. You needed to mix it with, get this, garlic. Get the mix right and you got this amazing, efficient bulb. Mix it wrong, and *kablooey*."

"That why the factory went out of business?"

"No. It was killed by the economy."

"What?"

"Think for a second. You make a light bulb that lasts forever. So everybody buys one." He raised a single finger, arched his eyebrows, and stared at me expectantly.

"But not two."

"Genius points!" Cliff said, and pretended to turn on a light bulb over my head.

I opened the diary again to jot down some notes on reidium. "That's weird." I had turned back to the notes I'd written that morning. "I was sure I'd underlined the word 'dossier.' But now it's all just faded, like I wrote it and then erased it."

Cliff looked at the page and shrugged. "Maybe the ink is cheap?"

I held up the heavy metal pen. "I don't know. This pen looks pretty expensive. And even cheap ink shouldn't fade *that* fast." The bell rang. I slid the diary into my backpack.

"So this hockey game is actually a big deal?" I said as we lined up to throw out our recycling.

"The whole town is going to be there, plus a ton of tourists. The mayor has declared it a city-wide holiday."

"Cool," I said, not really feeling it. I knew Dad loved hockey, but I just couldn't get too excited about fifty thousand people sitting in the cold screaming at a bunch of millionaires slapping a round piece of rubber. I mean, it's obviously not as cool as battling giants with flaming swords.

Right?

CHAPTER 5

EVEN MORE BIZARRE

Cliff stayed after school for band practice. I thanked him again for the tissues and promised I'd call once I got home since, and I think I've mentioned this bitterly, I still didn't have my own phone.

The snow had stopped, but enough had fallen to make it a bit of a slog getting home. I still didn't know how I was going to get inside. We didn't keep an extra key hidden anywhere.

When I got home, there were footprints starting in the middle of the driveway and leading to the house and back. But no tire tracks. It was like whoever had made the prints had appeared out of thin air and then vanished.

Dad and Mom were still supposed to be at work, but maybe one of them had come home early? The front door was slightly ajar. "Mom?" I called. "Dad?" No answer. "RigaTony?" No meow or screeching lunge at my face.

The snow began to fall again and a biting wind kicked up. There was a loud *bang* from above. I looked up. The clouds were mostly grey. But one spot seemed to be a kind of stained, muddy brown. There was another *bang*, and an eruption of brown smoke shot down from the sky, the wind quickly whooshing it away.

Sooty snow fell in flakes on the ground around me. *What the heck?* Then a chunk of something that looked like frozen cat poop (trust me, RigaTony has left me plenty of specimens for comparison) hit the driveway with a loud *clunk*.

I ran inside and locked the door. The house was eerily silent. I turned and gasped. The kitchen had been demolished. Drawers had been emptied out, dishes shattered. The microwave was leaning against the wall, bent and cracked. Bits of plate crunched under my feet. The living room was worse. The credenza with all my dad's favourite china had been knocked over, everything inside completely smashed. I had a horrible thought. Had my janitor come back to life and gone berserk after I'd left? Oh no.

I ran to the basement. Unlike the rest of the house, it was mostly untouched. Mostly. Someone had cut the cushions open. Stuffing had been thrown all over the place. I heard a pathetic *meow*. RigaTony, petrified with fear, crouched underneath the coffee table. I reached for him, but he hissed, then shot past me and up the stairs.

My computer rang. Dr. F. trying to make contact. Once I found my controller — under the couch — I clicked on "Answer."

Fassbinder began talking before I could say anything. "Jess! Thanks goodness. Are you okay?"

"Um . . ."

He hurried on, "I tried to reach your parents. No answer."

"They're still at work," I said dumbly.

"I've been trying there as well."

I started to panic. Clearly whatever was going on was way bigger than I'd imagined. "Dr. F., could they have been kidnapped? They aren't here and the house has been turned upside down."

"Okay, let's talk through this. Your parents were supposed to give you that dossier. Did they?"

"No one gave me anything but pancakes and tissues. Mom was super weird this morning and Dad was gone early."

"No mention of the file?"

"I bet that's what the robber was looking for, isn't it?"

"This dossier would be one of the most valuable things they own. Is there a safe in the house? Anywhere they might hide something like that?"

"They've never mentioned a safe."

"Anyplace else where no one would dare look?" He rubbed his balding head, clearly agitated.

Wait. I snapped my fingers. "Yes. There is."

"Hurry."

All of a sudden, a tiny gloved hand thrust a paper in Dr. F.'s face. "Requisition form," said a squeaky voice.

"Thanks, Jasper," he said. "Look, Jess. I'll fill this out and try to get you some help."

"You need to fill out a form to send help?"

He looked embarrassed, avoiding looking directly at me. "Budget cuts. Never mind. You need to find that dossier and get away. Do you understand?" I nodded. "Good luck," he said, then he hung up.

I ran. I knew the one place no robber would ever break into. My dad's secret hideaway, a place so foul nothing could survive there long. Only I, with my perpetually clogged proboscis, had ever dared even approach. His hockey equipment bag.

I rushed to the garage. I tried to flick on the light, but nothing happened. My eyes adjusted. Sure enough, tools, holiday decorations and old letters and tax returns were strewn all over the floor, along with the shattered remains of a light bulb. I avoided the glass and headed for the back wall.

Mom made him keep his equipment hung up by a hook in the vain hope it might air out. I ran my hand along the zipper. Someone *had* moved it, about five centimetres. I was impressed. When I'd tricked Cliff into trying to open the bag last summer he'd only moved the zipper half a centimetre before passing out.

I took a deep breath and unzipped it the entire way. The contents of the bag fell out like the insides of the Tauntaun after Han Solo sliced it with a lightsaber. Three spiders fell dead to the floor. One of the windowpanes cracked. Birds four blocks away took flight. Somewhere in the distance, a dog howled in agony.

But I stood oblivious to it all, nose stuffed, and saw the plastic bag Dad had taped to the bottom of the bag, underneath the rotting shin pads and unwashed socks. I pulled it out and ripped it open. Inside were two tickets to the outdoor game, an old cellphone, three hundred dollars, a signed Bobby Skull hockey card and a manila envelope with my name typed on the front. I stashed the money in my pocket along with the phone. I carefully placed the hockey card back in the plastic and tucked it inside the bag.

I turned over the envelope. There, written in incredibly tiny handwriting, were these words:

TOP SECRET
For: Jessica Flem
Open only on signs of specialness, uniquetitude or possible superpowering

I wasn't sure those were even words. I was just about to open the envelope when there was a *bang* from outside and a *clunk* as something fell onto the roof of the garage. I looked out the window just in time to see the rungs of a filthy rope ladder being lowered to the ground.

The robber was back. He or she must have been waiting for me to return. Stupidly, I'd led the robber right to the dossier.

Large black boots appeared on the ladder. There was no time to lose. I jammed the envelope in my jacket and hopped on my bike. I wasn't sure how fast or how far I could ride in the snow, but I was willing to bet it was faster and farther than I could run. I tried to steady my already uneven breathing. I took a hit off my blue puffer and got ready to open the door. Someone was crunching the snow outside.

"Boy could I use a Gorg to help me escape right now," I said, more as a joke to calm myself than anything else.

My nose tingled. I could feel something scratching and clawing at my nostril. In shock, I watched as a tiny green Gorg yanked itself out of my nose onto my upper lip. It saluted. Then it crawled down my front and began rummaging in my pocket, tearing up my used tissues. When it crawled back out again it was twice the size, and growing. The door began to rise.

"You and me together, butt for brains," I said. The Gorg nodded, leaped onto the handlebars, and crouched down. I'd head for Garvia Greep's house. As creepy as she was, she was the only person my parents had ever trusted with my life.

The door opened more and more, revealing a figure

completely covered in black military-style clothes, their face covered with a ski mask.

"Not today, Commandude!" I began pedalling furiously. Commandude stayed rooted to the spot, arms spread wide. I swerved slightly to avoid the arms, and my front tire connected with a right knee. Commandude fell backward with a howl. The Gorg leaped from the bike, spitting blue flames onto the ski mask, which began to burn.

I sped away, but stole a look back. A decrepit old blimp was hovering barely three metres above the house. It was brown, poop brown, with huge grey patches sewn into the fabric. It was clearly leaking both gas and smoke and seemed unable to make up its mind whether to stay afloat or just give up and let gravity finish it off.

Commandude was punching at the pestering Gorg, who avoided the fists and then tore the ski mask off. I gasped. Garvia Greep! She saw me and ran, the Gorg literally licking at her heels. The blimp began turning in the air, its nose cone slowly angling in my direction. I could see the pilot's cabin. The wheel was turning, but there was no one there!

I turned and pumped my legs as fast as I could, my lungs feeling like they were going to explode. I had to find Cliff and I needed to find him fast. Luckily, I knew exactly where he was.

CHAPTER 6

HOT AIR

Mom once told me that there was no worse sound in the world than a duck being strangled by a chicken. Except, she said, Cliff practising trumpet. I didn't ask how she knew about the first thing, but I had experienced the second.

Cliff sometimes dropped by the house to show off his latest embouchure exercises. Paint had peeled. Windows had shattered. Cockroaches had fled. The dead were raised. It was like the audio version of Dad's hockey equipment. Let's leave it at that.

So I knew that he was still at band practice when I cycled around the corner of the school and saw our music teacher, Miss Terioso, on the stairs, weeping. The school band was scheduled to play at the big game and they were all polished and ready, except for the one-person brass section. Cliff. (One benefit of being the only person in town who owns a trumpet is that they kind of have to let you in the band.)

I looked back to see if the blimp was close. It wasn't. Greep had been battling the Gorg and eventually escaped by grabbing the rope ladder. The blimp almost crashed from the extra weight and had to stop and hover for a few minutes, spewing and backfiring. But that had given me the time I needed to put some distance between them and me. The Gorg had watched me pedal away, then dissolved into a green puddle of slime right in the middle of the road.

I slid the bike to a stop, jumped off, handed Miss T. a handful of (I think) unused tissues, and ran inside. The rest of the band members were huddling together in the hallway. A noise like a cow being tortured came from the music room.

I took a deep breath and pushed open the double doors. Cliff, his cheeks as red as apples, was doing his best to push something resembling music out of the end of his horn. He was failing. He saw me and stopped. The sigh of relief from the rest of the band formed its own jet stream. I walked in and let the doors close.

"We gotta go," I said.

"But I need to practise."

"No kidding. But I don't have time to explain, and we need to get out of here right now."

"But band practice goes for another hour!"

"I guess we'll have to come up with a clever excuse to bail," I said, "because I need your help." I fixed him again with the best best-friend stare. This time it only took two seconds.

"Okay." He nodded and picked up his trumpet case.

Just then Miss T. opened the doors. "Is it over?" she asked, a huge grin breaking across her wet cheeks.

"Almost got it. But . . ." Cliff said, giving me a wink, "I'm going to head over to Jess's place to do some more practise. If that's okay?"

"Yes, yes, fine," she said, shooing us out the door with one hand and waving the rest of the band back in with the other. The music room doors slammed shut behind us with the unmistakable sound of a deadbolt being locked.

"Cliff to the rescue! Charge!" he said, then bleated something on his horn that might, in an alternate universe, have been what they call a fanfare.

There was a sob from the other side of the door, and a *thump* like someone banging their forehead against solid wood. "I think she's impressed," Cliff said.

"It's pronounced *de*-pressed," I said. "Look. I've got

my bike out front, and the Grim Greeper is chasing me with a murderous look in her eyes."

"Seriously?" Cliff said, putting his trumpet into its case.

"Yeah. But I was able to fend her off with a snot Gorg."

"Wait, YOU DID IT AGAIN?"

"Yeah. Weird."

"It's pronounced AWESOME!"

"I seem to be able to do it only once in a while," I said. "It's exasperating. But I might have some leads on why it's happening." I opened my jacket and showed him a corner of the envelope.

"That shirt does not look comfortable," he said.

"It's an envelope, you bonehead."

"Still doesn't look comfortable."

"Ugh. Look. This is an envelope my parents were supposed to give me in case I showed any sign of, I dunno, special powers. Greep tore up my house looking for it."

"Let me guess . . . was it hidden in the shoulder pads?" He shuddered at the memory. "Please don't say the jockstrap."

"Shin pads, luckily. Wait . . ." Something wasn't right.

"What isn't right?" Cliff asked.

"When I tore open the plastic wrap, there were two tickets to the big game inside."

"Cool!"

"But Mom said Dad was out lining up for tickets this morning. Why would he line up if he already had the tickets?"

"Okay. So maybe your mom was lying?"

"I dunno," I said. "I'm worried. Fassbinder says he hasn't been able to reach either of them. Do you think they might have been kidnapped?"

"But you said your mom drove off on her own."

"Yeah, but with no coat or purse. It was like she was hypnotized." I began hyperventilating again, taking a shot from my almost-empty puffer.

"Don't get ahead of yourself," Cliff said, putting a hand on my shoulder. "Stay calm. Stick to the evidence. Got any?"

I nodded, calming down. "I've been keeping notes." I pulled the diary out of my coat pocket.

"Okay. So what do we have to go on so far? Give me everything."

I thumbed through my notes. "I have a superpower."

"GOO-per power, you mean."

"Whatever. Greep is out to get this file, and maybe me. She might already have my parents. Dr. F. says he was expecting me to have superpowers, but I don't even know how to control them, or how they work."

"But the uncomfortable-looking file might help."

"I hope."

I pulled out my dad's old cellphone. I tried to turn it on but the battery was dead. "And I'll also need to find a charger for this asap."

"To try calling your parents."

"Um. Yeah. That, and other stuff."

Cliff narrowed his eyes. His eyebrows were like two caterpillars kissing. "You want the phone to log on to your Gang of Geeks game, don't you?"

"Well, maybe. But I'll try calling my parents *first*."

"Nice to see you have your priorities in order."

"I'm just being prepared for everything!" I said, offended. "The G of G playdowns start soon. I have to be ready."

He shook his head. "Fine." He relaxed. The caterpillars took a breather. "So what's our mission?"

"Find my parents. Then find out what's going on with my nose. Then win the G of G tournament."

"And help me practise trumpet."

"Sure. Whatever. Definitely in that order." Our conversation was interrupted by a loud *bang* from outside. "And figure out what's going on with that blimp."

"Blimp?"

I pointed outside. The poop-coloured blimp was about a hundred metres away, spewing even more smoke. It was bouncing off the road and back up again, a little like a slow-motion basketball.

"That thing puts the 'limp' in 'blimp,'" Cliff said. "How is it even airborne?"

"It's still dangerous," I said. The blimp stopped, hovering over my bike. The rope ladder unfurled. "We'll have to go out the back."

"The parking lot is wide open back there," Cliff said. It was true. The parking lot backed on to the school. There was a field and a playground, but nowhere to hide if we were spotted.

"We just have to sprint," I said. A pair of black boots began descending from the side of the cockpit. Greep. "Go! It's our only chance."

We ducked down to avoid being seen and ran as fast as we could down the corridor. I stole looks out the windows a few times as we hurried, seeing snippets of what was happening, like flashes of action in a movie trailer.

Greep picked up my bike and *sniffed* it! We ran. I peeked again. She was gone.

"Shoot!" I said, ducking back down. Had she seen me? Sniffed me out? We turned a corner and sprinted out the back door.

The doors banged shut behind us. No. The banging was coming from in front of us. I looked up. A giant trash bin was hovering over our heads.

"We're going to be crushed!" I said, throwing up my hands to defend myself.

"It's just garbage day," Cliff yelled. He grabbed my arm and pulled it down. "See?"

A giant green truck had grabbed the bin with two large hooks and was dumping the contents into its back. It lowered the empty bin back down to the ground. The driver backed up to slot the hooks into the other large bin.

"Okay, we make a run for it through the parking lot," I said.

But before we could move, Greep came around the corner of the building. She smiled her sweetest fake smile. "Jessiekins," she said. "I'm here to help! Just stay right there." She sprinted toward us.

"Jessiekins!" Cliff started laughing.

"Shut up," I said. She was just a couple of metres away. There was only one chance to escape. I grabbed Cliff's arm. "Trust me?"

"No," he said.

I frowned but held on to him as I clutched the edge of the garbage bin. The truck lifted it up, and Cliff and I were swung up and over and into the back of the truck. We landed on a pile of thick plastic bags. Luckily it wasn't one of those trash-compacting monster trucks. Just a really disgusting slimy one.

Cliff started gagging. The truck lowered the bin.

"We're safe!" I yelled. "Ha, ha!"

Cliff was too busy holding his hands up to his mouth to answer, but I think he was relieved.

There was a loud *clank*. Greep's hand reached over the side. The driver must not have seen her because he continued backing up. Her other hand appeared next to the first as the truck began turning to drive away.

"Do something!" I yelled, more at myself than at Cliff, who had turned about as green as the slime on the walls of the truck. He tried to move but stumbled and fell.

I looked around for anything I could use, a crowbar or stick. Nothing.

Then I saw Cliff's trumpet case. I grabbed it and ran over to Greep. I smacked the case down hard on her hands. The case bent at an odd angle as I smacked her again. To be honest, I think I hit the metal side of the bin more than her hands, but with a howl she finally let go and fell.

She rolled away into a snowbank on the side of the road. Then the truck turned a corner and she disappeared from view. The blimp, still struggling, was way off in the distance. It began to rise into the low clouds.

Cliff came over. He'd found an old clothespin somewhere in the pile and had pinched his nose shut as best he could.

"Not being able to smell is your real superpower," Cliff said. Then he spied the case. "No. No! NOOOO!!"

"Sorry, Cliff," I said, handing it back to him. No question, the bent case contained a bent trumpet.

Cliff didn't say anything as he slowly unzipped the soft outer lining and pulled out the silver instrument. The horn was bent upward at a forty-five-degree angle. The pipe for the mouthpiece was twisted sideways. It looked like a kindergartner's drawing of a trumpet.

"Look, Cliff, I . . ."

He held up his hand to stop me. A tear ran down his cheek. He gave a loud, sad sniff, brought the trumpet to his lips, and blew. And, on a day of weird miracles and strange occurrences, what came out was actually music.

CHAPTER 7

NOW WHAT?

"Now what?" Cliff said.

"Keep running."

"Like your nose?"

I hit him in the head with a cabbage. We were sitting on a giant pile of garbage in the Dimly dump. Luckily, most of the trash was in bags or boxes, or frozen, so our clothes weren't getting too disgusting.

"Shouldn't we head back?" Cliff asked, shivering slightly.

"Not yet." I nervously scanned the sky for any sign of the blimp.

Cliff said something else. Something about, "So why not just go to the ... *muffle, muffle*?" He still had a clothespin attached to his nose and he'd torn one of my tissues in half and jammed the bits up his nose. He was not easy to understand.

"What did you say?"

I said, "'So why not just go to the —?'"

"To the bumblebees? To the Christmas trees?"

He pulled the bits out of his nose. "The authorities! Why not just go to THE COPS?"

"Oh," I said. "I don't have a charged phone. And, think. Two kids phone the police and report that a large, farting blimp is chasing them because I can make Gorgs come out of my nose." I cocked my head.

"Yeah. Okay. Got it."

"If we're lucky they won't charge *us* with making a prank call."

"So let's go to my house. Dad won't be home until later."

"We can't go to your house. Greep saw us together. It's the first place she'll look." I pulled (what I hope was) an old shirt from the garbage and wiped my nose. "I wish I had a troll to fight for me," I said. Nothing. I threw away the cloth.

"Nice work, Aladdin," Cliff said. "Maybe your goober genie only grants three gross wishes."

"Ha, ha," I said.

"No. I'm being serious. It makes as much sense as anything else that's been happening. Rub any lamps lately?"

"No. Well. I kind of broke one. But it wasn't magic. My dad had made it from a kit, using some old Splotnik bottle."

"Splotnik?"

I just shrugged. "That's what it said."

"Sounds fake. Maybe Dad will know." Cliff pulled out his cellphone. Yes . . . his cellphone.

"You've had a phone all this time!" I threw another cabbage but he ducked. "Can I use it?" I held out my hand.

He began typing. "In a second. I'm just going to text my dad first to let him know."

"Know what?"

"That there's a crazed babysitter in a ghost blimp who's looking for us. And that he might want to lock the front door."

I watched as he texted "cave!"

"Cave?"

"It's pronounced CAH-vay. It's Latin."

"For what?"

Cliff just sighed and kept typing. "Non responde ostium! postea invocabo."

"What the heck does that mean?"

"It's a little trick Dad and I use when we don't want anyone to know what we're saying."

"It works."

"I typed 'Beware. Don't answer the door. Will call later.' in Latin."

"I'll take your word for it."

"Fine. Stay ignorant." He handed me the phone. I began typing. In English. Cliff looked over and frowned. "Are you seriously using my data to log on to that game?"

"I need to check something," I said. I wasn't totally lying. I was half hoping that Gary might have sent me another message on G of G. But no answer from him yet. I quickly checked my status update. There were still six days, twenty-three hours and twelve minutes until the start of my first battle. *Squeal, squeal,* went the phone. Cliff glared at me.

"The laser pig is practically begging me to fight!" I grumbled. With one more swipe I lopped off the pig's head and grabbed the measly twenty points. "I need to stay sharp."

"Give me that phone." He reached for it, but I dodged him just as Fairfax began sprinting up a mountain.

"I'd like to get off this dump NOW!" Cliff yelled.

"Fine." I closed the window. I tried calling my mom. No answer. Dad. No answer. I sighed.

"What is Dr. F.'s number?" Cliff asked.

"I have no idea."

"Maybe it's inside the envelope?"

The envelope! I'd forgotten all about it. I unzipped my coat, tore open the envelope, and pulled out a bunch of wrinkled yellow sheets of paper. I took a deep breath. Cliff did too, then gagged and re-stuffed his nose with tissue bits.

This is what the pages said.

Dimly General Hospital
From: Dr. Edgar Fassbinder
To: Nurse Debbie Nussbaum
Patient: Jessica Flem

Born with unusually strong lungs, her ability to breathe on her own was noted during delivery. The events of the thirteenth of last month have changed the situation dramatically. Far from enhancing Flem's bronchial or pulmonary capacity, the reidium exposure seems to have done the opposite.

Given the advanced mental capabilities reidium has produced in lab mice, this is most peculiar. Of course, there has also been a corresponding demand for expensive gourmet cheese. (Monetary matters are not to be sneezed at, if you'll excuse the pun. Patient Flem has already exhausted the hospital's supply of tissues.

And her parents' litigious nature in this case is putting a further strain on our finances.)

There are slight signs of improvement. After days of what could be termed "decline," the patient's lungs have stabilized and even begun to improve. It's as if the lungs themselves have begun to evolve to deal with the internal changes. Most interesting.

<u>Future mutation is possible. Indeed, I would speculate that it is probable.</u> Yearly checkups are recommended. For all four patients.

Dr. Edgar Fassbinder
Chief Medical Officer, Dimly General Hospital

So. My parents knew there was something weird about me right from the start. I blew my nose. This stupid nose goo thing wasn't natural. It was a curse. And, for some reason, now that I was a teenager, it had decided to go rogue.

And I was just one of four "patients." I had a pretty good idea who the others were.

"This sucks," I said.

"There's more," Cliff said. He pointed down. There was a note from my parents.

TO: The Board of Directors, Dimly General
     Hospital
FROM: The Parents of Jessica Flem

We understand that the effects of the electrical storm earlier this year were unexpected and unpredictable.

We would like to thank the Dimly General Hospital staff for their help, particularly the efforts of Nurse Nussbaum (may she rest in peace) and her able assistant, Garvia Greep, in easing us through this worrisome time.

The large cash settlement will be held in trust until such time as Jess turns thirteen. At that point the account will be put under her control, with our legal oversight. The necessary paperwork will remain in a bank vault until her thirteenth birthday. The need for parental oversight will expire four years from that date. If anything happens to us before that time, we ask that Garvia Greep be given power of attorney and guardianship rights.

Dr. Fassbinder has recommended yearly consultations to monitor Jess's reaction to whatever happened to her on that horrible night. Even Jess will not be made aware of the peculiar circumstances of her first days here on earth until such time as events force us to reveal the truth. We hope that day never comes.

Yours truly,
Gardenia and Jim Flem

I leaned back on a garbage bag, the papers loose in my hands, mentally exhausted.

The green people I could conjure up — radioactive boogers, whatever you want to call them — Dr. F. and my parents had been waiting for them to happen. And my parents were now in grave danger. If they were out of the way, Greep would get me. If I were out of the way, Greep would get the money.

This still left a lot of questions. Like, if Greep was after my money, why was she coming after me in a pilotless blimp? But the main pieces were falling into place. I was the prize. Either for my money or my mucus. And I was darned if Greep or anyone else would get their hands on those.

"Get their hands on your mucus? Nice image," Cliff said.

"How did you know about that?"

"You were thinking out loud."

"Sorry. Okay. Time to start fighting back." I felt like Fairfax the Elfling. Greep the Gruesome had just attacked. It was time to titanium-up my fist and slug her in the face.

"Slugs with faces. Nice image," Cliff said, chuckling. "Thinking out loud again?"

"Yeah. But I'm with you. Let's go."

CHAPTER 8

GOING, GOING, GORG

We slunk around through the trees that separated the dump from the main part of town. The trees kept the worst smells from travelling into town when the winds changed. At least, that's what Cliff said, and I trusted his sensitive nose more than my stuffed one.

I kept looking up, expecting the blimp to swing into view at any moment. So far, nothing but snowflakes and birds. I pulled out my diary. Before we'd set out, I'd drawn a map of the best route back to town, with a big *X* over Mom's flower shop. Finding Dad was more problematic. He was a freelance accountant, which meant he was mostly on the road, and could be anywhere with almost any client. I'd left messages, just in case he wasn't answering because the screen showed it was Cliff calling. But, so far, no response.

"If we keep to the trees, then sneak around the alleys, we have a good chance of getting to Mom's place unnoticed."

"Might take us a little longer than heading straight there," Cliff said, running his finger along the route.

"Longer, but safer," I said.

We reached the edge of the trees and huddled behind a snow-covered bush. Dimly Field, site of the upcoming game, was to our right across a huge, open parking lot.

"Look. They're setting up the rink," Cliff said, pointing to a line of trucks. Sure enough, workers were lifting huge squares of SynthetICE off the flatbeds and carrying them onto what was usually the Dimly football field. We could see them through the opened gates, slipping the parts together like puzzle pieces.

"That is so awesome!" Cliff said. "Science just makes the world better."

I blew my nose for the 100000000000000th time that afternoon. "Sometimes," I said, bitterly.

"Well, all I know is that if I could make my nose gunk fight battles for me, I'd consider myself a superhero."

"Maybe. If I knew why it worked sometimes and snot others."

"You said 'snot others'!"

"No, I didn't."

Cliff was laughing so hard he couldn't even talk. He just held his stomach, pointed at me, and nodded.

"Shhhhh," I said, looking around nervously. But the noise of all the trucks and hammering was plenty loud enough to drown us out. Or, I realized, the sound of an approaching Zeppelin. Cliff apparently saw it as an opportunity to pull his trumpet out of its case. "Are you *trying* to get caught?"

"I'm not going to play it. I just want to see it again. I was supposed to play it during the game. There's no way Miss T. will let me play now."

"You played it way better like this."

"You think so?"

"You really can't hear how the music sounds, can you?"

He shrugged. "Dad says I'm tone deaf. Of course, he's usually wearing headphones when I'm practising, so I don't know how he'd know." We were interrupted by the hum of a blimp coming in low over the horizon.

"Oh no!" I said. "She found us!"

Cliff narrowed his eyes and peered into the clouds. "No. That's a different blimp." He turned his attention back to the horn.

The blimp turned, and I could see that it was almost the exact opposite of the dumpy thing that had been chasing us. This one was sleek and white, with a big ad painted on the side: *Visit Dimly: The Best Dim Place in the World!*

"That is the dumbest, or should I say dimmest, town slogan in the world," I said. "And why is there a blimp here anyway?"

"They fly over and film some of the game. The bird's-eye view. You know, like they do at big football games on TV. It's like the overhead view of *Gang of Greats.*"

"How do you even know about that?"

"I've seen you play it a thousand times," he said, but his eyes darted around in a kind of funny way.

"I guess that makes sense." Even the mention of the game made my fingers twitch. If I didn't keep up my practice I'd be way too rusty to beat even a Level-Two Troll like Gary.

The blimp was doing lazy, graceful circles over the stadium. "It's kinda pretty," I said.

"And, unlike the one chasing us, this one doesn't seem to fart." Then he played a loud *toot* on his horn and gave me the goofiest smile ever. How do you not laugh at that? I ask you. Still, the preparations for the game were louder than we were.

"We should get moving," Cliff said, wiping tears from his eyes.

Small flakes of snow fell on his brown tuque, like sugar dusting on a chocolate lava cake. He suddenly looked . . . cute.

"You gonna puke?" he said.

"What? Why?"

"I don't know. You had this weird look on your face and you were staring at me."

Despite the cold, I felt my cheeks warm. What had gotten into me? "I'm just glad to have you here, as a friend," I mumbled.

"It's pronounced sidekick." He grinned.

"What?"

"Every superhero needs a sidekick. Batman had Robin. Superman had some weird radioactive dog I think."

"And we would be?"

"Booger-Girl and Toots!" He gave another blow on his horn.

I shook my head sadly. "C'mon, Toots. I think we'll just have to risk sprinting across the parking lot."

Just then one of the empty trucks began driving on the road toward us. "Or we can hitch a ride," I said. "AND save some time." The truck turned a corner and slowed almost to a stop. "Trust me?" I asked.

"Still no," he said.

I grabbed Cliff's hand as I ran to the side of the road and then, just as the truck was about to speed up again, we jumped on the back. Another truck pulled into view behind us.

"In here," Cliff said. There was a large blue tarp, and we slid underneath. Our truck rumbled on. We hadn't been spotted.

"Can I see your phone again?" My fingers were clearly twitching as I reached my hand toward him.

"Booger-Girl, this is just sad."

"What?"

"Gamer withdrawal. Tsk, tsk."

"I just need to see if anyone's sent me a message!"

"Yeah, right." But he handed it over.

I logged on to my G of G page. Still no message from Gary, or from beancounter3000x. I sent Gary a response, finally, saying I'd been having an interesting day too, and agreeing we should talk. Then I started fighting a magic Marauding Magpie (it drops radioactive poop bombs), but my heart wasn't totally in it. Of course, I wasn't going to say no to the gold coin I got once I squashed it with my power-glove of death.

Just as the feathers began to disintegrate, a Gruntasaurus rose from the ground and bared its claws. Way more valuable. I sat up straighter and flexed my thumbs. "Now we're talking," I said. But before I could even prep a magic arrow, an ad popped up on the screen. Stupid mobile version. "This doesn't happen at home."

"Home. Sounds like a dream," Cliff said.

The screen was filled with a boy's face. He was standing on a beach. The wind gently rustled his hair. He looked sort of familiar, friendly. No, more than friendly . . . amazing.

I don't even remember the first few words he spoke, except it was like an angel singing. He was saying something about remembering to buy lots and lots and lots of Chompo chocolate bars. Lots. My stomach rumbled in response. I realized I hadn't eaten in hours, and that had been half of Cliff's dead-fish-and-cheese sandwich.

"He's so right!" I said. The ad ended. I wanted to play it again, and again . . . but it had disappeared. All I knew was that I needed Chompo chocolate and I needed it now.

"Wasn't that Archie? Belinda's cousin or something. He was in town last summer."

"Archie," I said. "We were babies together! What a wonderful name. And his voice . . . !"

"Sounded like a chipmunk chewing bubble gum to me."

I tapped Cliff's trumpet case. "Toots. You need to get those ears checked. He's awesome."

Cliff shrugged. "I hear what I hear. And I've had that chocolate. Tastes like brown sawdust."

The truck slowed as we approached town, and I jumped off at a stop sign.

"Hey, where are you going?" Cliff yelled.

"I need chocolate!" I called. "Race you to Biscotti's corner store!" Cliff jumped off just in time and chased after me.

For some reason the idea of finding my mother had completely evaporated.

CHAPTER 9

CHOCOLATE BARRED

The neon sign in the front window of Biscotti's corner store blazed like a ray of sunshine on a stormy day. "Chompo," I whispered, then yelled louder and louder as I approached the front door.

"What has gotten into you?" Cliff asked, huffing as he caught up to me.

"Nothing yet," I said, smacking my empty stomach. "But soon . . . ambrosia!"

"It's junky fundraiser milk chocolate!"

I walked through the door, the jingling of the bell sounding like the laughter of fairies. (This is what Cliff tells me I said, anyway. I'm not 100 percent sure he's telling the truth.) The chocolates lay in a cardboard box on the counter.

I rushed over, squealing with delight (apparently). "Hark! Their golden wrappers do gleam like a pot of gold at the end of a rainbow!" (Again, blame Cliff for this "memory." I do.) A handwritten sign next to the box said, *All proceeds go to help the homeless.*

Mr. Biscotti seemed just as excited as I was. "I saw the ad online and I just knew I needed to help. I bought three bars myself! There are only five left."

I laid down a fifty-dollar bill and bought the whole lot. "Oh, happy day! If I were a fluffy puppy I would wag my tail!" I (according to Cliff) said. I tore off the golden wrapper and took a bite. Tears of joy poured down my face.

"Oh! Archie! Archie! You were right! How I love you! Kissy, kissy!" (Cliff is definitely misremembering *that* bit.)

As I stood there eating my third Chompo bar, which wasn't as bad as Cliff says, the spell broke. I stopped chewing. "Why did I buy five of these again?" I asked. I felt slightly ill. Cliff shrugged. So did Mr. Biscotti.

"I guess I need to send the money," he said. "Although . . . ten bucks a chocolate bar seems a bit much."

"Can I get a partial refund?" I asked, shoving the uneaten bars his way.

"I'm afraid I already rang it in to my system," Mr. Biscotti said. "Which reminds me: your mom and dad were in here about an hour ago."

I started. "What? Together?"

He nodded. "Your dad was helping me with my taxes when your mom walked in with a rose. She told him to have a sniff. Then, all of a sudden, he just stood up and walked out. He left everything behind." He lifted my dad's briefcase up from behind the counter and placed it on top. "Cellphone. Datebook. Tax code booklets. Wallet."

I looked at the phone. All my messages were still unread and unheard. Ditto for a bunch of calls from Dr. F. Everything else looked normal. Messy and boring, but normal. His meticulously detailed datebook said he was supposed to finish Mr. Biscotti's taxes and then head to the bank.

"The bank!" I looked at Cliff. "My parents' letter said, '*The necessary paperwork will remain in a bank vault until her thirteenth birthday.*'"

"Once that account gets signed over to you, it's game over," Cliff said. "Greep can get rid of your parents, and then she becomes your guardian and personal banker."

"Mr. Biscotti, did they take the rose with them?"

"Nope. It's in the garbage over there," he said. "Your

dad just let it drop on the floor. I swept it up but didn't want to risk touching it. Bad vibe."

I rushed over. The rose was covered by dozens of golden Chompo chocolate bar wrappers.

"How many of those did you sell?" Cliff asked.

"About three hundred." He suddenly banged his head with his palm. "I forget to charge the sales tax!"

"That's a lot of moolah," Cliff said. Mr. B. sobbed.

I grabbed the rose from the bottom of the can. It was identical to the roses Mom had put in front of me at breakfast. "Cliff, I need you to take a very quick whiff and tell me what you smell."

He walked over but I put up my hand to stop him. "Not too close. If this does what I think it does, we need to be careful."

Cliff took a sniff. "It smells like a rose, but with some other flowers in there too." He grimaced. "And some burnt rubber with . . . cat pee? Yuck."

Then his eyes started to go all buggy and he wobbled slightly. I tossed the rose back in the can and covered it with wrappers. I rushed to Cliff and started waving my hand in front of his face to dispel the aroma.

"Cliff, you okay?"

"Yeah," he shook his head. His eyes took a second to focus. "It's like there was some sort of fog that started to make stuff all, I don't know, foggy."

"Very eloquent. Try it in Latin next time."

He gave his head a shake and the effects seemed to wear off. "Wow. That's some fowerful plower."

"Greep showed up with roses this morning. That's how she put my mom under her spell! She tried it with me but my nose gooped up." I turned back to Mr. Biscotti. "Any idea where they went?"

"They just said they had some business to attend to."

I knew what *business* meant. "They are at the bank," I said, and I was sure of it.

"Shouldn't we check your mom's shop first?"

I thought for a second, tapping my hand on the counter. "Maybe we should split up and do both."

I opened my diary to the map. I pointed at Mom's shop and then drew a big *T*. "Toots, you go there and then I'll run here." I was about to draw a big *B-G* over the bank when I hesitated, my pen hovering right over the page. The *T* I'd *just* drawn was fading right before my eyes. I paused, then drew a large *B-G* on Mr. Biscotti's store instead.

"You're going to stay here?" Cliff asked.

"No. I am going to the bank. But I have a hunch about this diary." I turned to Mr. Biscotti. "If anyone comes here looking for me, can you stall them as long as possible?"

"Of course. But in return can you do me one favour?"

"Sure. What?"

"Don't mention the missing tax to your dad."

CHAPTER 10

BANK ON IT

I kept my back flat against the wall of Dimly's book/ farm feed store (Words 'n' Herds), and peered around the corner. The First National Bank of Manitoba was right across the street. Mr. Biscotti had said that my parents had left for the bank about an hour earlier. But Dad's datebook said they weren't expecting him until around now.

And if there was one thing I knew about our bank, thanks to numerous rants from my dad, it was that nothing there ever happened quickly. He often called it the First National Bank of ManiSLOWba. So there was still a chance that, if they were inside, they hadn't finished whatever paperwork they needed to fill out.

The sun was setting on the horizon. The street lights

were just starting to flicker on. My phone buzzed. A text from Cliff: "Florist clausa est, desolata et tenebrica."

Ugh. "I DON'T KNOW LATIN, DOOFUS!" I messaged back.

My phone buzzed again. "Doofus at least looks like a Latin word. Ur learning."

"Grrr," I typed.

"It means 'Florist is closed, empty, dark.'"

"Cool."

"Blimp overhead. Dipping down like sick fish. Wait . . ." The phone stayed silent for a good minute. I stared at the screen, my fingers tense. Finally, words flashed: "Door opening. Dark figure slipping out. Heading toward Biscotti!"

I texted, "I knew it." Greep had been waiting for us to show up at Mom's shop because that's what I'd written in the diary. I don't know how, but that diary was sending Greep everything I wrote down. It wouldn't take her long to realize we weren't at the store. Time for me to move.

My phone buzzed one more time with a text from Cliff: "Will sneak a look inside while Greep away."

I ran across the intersection and pushed open the front door of the bank. The bright gold of the ceiling momentarily blinded me.

"Can I help you, Jess?" It was a man's voice.

I blinked until my eyes adjusted. Cliff's dad! He was standing near the front door, wearing a large coat, looking around like he was lost. "I'm looking for my parents," I said, my body trembling with a mix of fear and hope about what he would say next.

"Ah, yes. They seem to be involved in some lengthy discussion, nay, argument with the manager, Mr. Kinew."

"YES!" I said, jumping in the air. They were still here!

Mr. Snuffington the Second tilted his head. "I'm not sure it's going well. All the tellers and staff have already gone home so they are burning the midnight oil, as it were. I think I was about to do some banking of my own . . . But then, why . . . ?" His voice trailed off.

"Ah," I said, not really listening. My feet were already turning toward the interior of the bank.

He tapped my shoulder. "By the way, have you seen Heathcliff? He sent me a very *aliena* message."

"Aliens?"

"No, no. It's Latin for *strange*. My apologies. I do slip into that. He said to be careful . . . and then I went outside . . . or I was going to . . ."

Was he going to ramble on forever? I cut him off. "Cliff should be here soon."

"Wonderful," he said. Then he took a seat on a

bench in the foyer, his eyes still darting all around. "I shall attend his arrival with the utmost expectancy."

"Um. Okay?" I walked away. The manager's office was in a glass-walled cubicle near the back.

I could hear Mom's voice. She sounded calm but was clearly having a discussion with the manager that was not going the way she wanted. "Mr. Julius Clark Kinew," she said. Wow. She'd used HIS full name. "I know this is irregular but we are simply asking that you release control of this account to Garvia Greep."

"See how we crossed out our names and wrote hers on the form." My father! He said it in a monotone. I could hear him tapping his finger on the desk.

"Yes, well, Mr. and Mrs. Flem," Mr. Kinew said, "I realize that you are long-standing customers, but without your proper legal identification, I just can't do that."

"You know who we are," Dad said, pronouncing each word slowly.

"Well, ahem, I know who you SAY you are. But, to be frank, you are acting a little . . . bizarre. Nevertheless, without any corroborating documents, I'm afraid I just cannot take your word for it."

Of course! Mom had forgotten her purse at home, and Dad's wallet was in my pocket. Mr. Kinew was a stickler for procedure. He once made me sort the coins from my lemonade stand by value AND year before he let me deposit them.

"Sign." Dad slapped the table.

"I am sorry. But procedures must be followed. Especially when it concerns such a . . ." He gave a little cough. ". . . *substantial* amount of money."

"We are giving you one more chance," Dad and Mom said together. It sounded way creepy. Things were about to get hairy in there. I needed to do something.

I walked into the cubicle, holding my dad's wallet above my head. "Looking for this?" I hoped hearing my voice might snap them back to reality.

Nope. My parents turned around slowly, their eyes slightly glazed over like the lethargic sheep at the Dimly Petting Zoo.

"Jess," Mom said, her eyes blinking, but just a little. "Are you hungry for more pancakes?"

"Pancakes?"

Dad nodded slowly. "Yes, Jess. Have more pancakes." He started to walk toward me.

"Jessica?" Mr. Kinew stared at me from behind my dad. "Are you aware of what your parents are trying to do?"

"You have no idea how much weirdness is actually going on, Mr. K.," I said. Mom was walking toward him. Dad was now just steps away from me. I wanted to hug him, or maybe slap him, but he looked so strange. I threw his wallet at him, but he let it bounce off his belly and fall.

"I have a present for you." Dad pulled a pink rose out of his coat pocket. He waved it at my face.

"No!" I yelled, but my voice was drowned out by a sudden *crash* from the front of the bank. A chunk of what I assume was part of the oak doors smashed into the chandelier above Mr. Kinew's desk, sending sparks flying. Bits of shattered glass and electrical wire fell around me like snow. I started sneezing.

"This is a *latrocinium*," said a man's voice. "I mean, robbery."

CHAPTER 11

LAT-IN TROUBLE

Cliff's dad was holding up the bank?!

Then I heard Cliff's voice and my heart fell. "Give us all your *pecunia*. I mean, money." A blast shattered more chandeliers and plaster. "Booger-Girl. You will not escape if you do not give us your money. None of you will."

I slumped to the floor. Wait, was Cliff helping Greep this whole time?

Mr. Kinew was cowering under his desk. He was calling the police. Mom and Dad stood as still as trees, even as more debris littered the floor.

"Give up B-G," Cliff said.

"And make sure your parents sign the papers," Cliff's dad said.

The papers? Cliff had told him? I looked up. Mom and Dad were leaning over Mr. K.'s desk. They were signing the papers. And Dad was faking Mr. Kinew's signature! I tried to stand, but Mom put her hand on my head and pushed me back to the floor.

"The papers are signed," Mom and Dad said together.

"Not by me they're not," Mr. Kinew yelled from under the desk. A blast from somewhere in the foyer shattered the glass partition over Mr. Kinew's head.

"*Brutum fulmen*, Mr. Kinew," said Cliff's dad. "An empty threat."

"*Mortui non dicent*," Cliff added. "A dead man can tell no tales."

Another blast struck even closer, tearing a chunk off Mr. K.'s desk and sending his green banker's lamp smashing to the floor. A piece of glass cut my hand and I yelped in pain. Mr. K. had just plain fainted now. This couldn't be happening. I was all alone, surrounded by zombie-robot versions of my family and a traitorous friend and his pedantic pop.

Then I heard Garvia Greep's unmistakable voice. "Jessiekins! Are you inside? I'm here to help you! Come out of your hiding place!"

My head swam with confusion. Who was my friend? Who was my enemy?

"Come out now. My blimp is just outside. We can

escape together. Mr. Snuffington is trying to hold up the bank!"

"You're lying!" I called.

"No. It's true! It's all being caught on security cameras! Your poor parents aren't here, are they? I'd hate to see them hurt as innocent bystanders in a shootout. It would be tragic, but in no way suspicious." She chuckled.

"You rat!" I yelled.

I caught a glimpse of Cliff's dad through the doorway. He was holding what looked like a water squirter. He pulled the trigger. A blast of energy shot out, shattering a window in the domed ceiling. He tried to fire again, but the blaster started smoking. He looked at it, confused, then let it fall. He kept staring at it in a daze, as it began to melt. It was the same look my mom had had cooking pancakes. He wasn't working with Greep. Somehow she'd zapped him and turned him into a zombie too. Was that also true of Cliff?

"Stupid Department C equipment," Greep hissed. "Next time steal a real gun, not some cheap government-issue knock-off!" I couldn't tell who she was talking to, but I prayed it wasn't Cliff. An electronic squawk answered back, "Just finish the job. Then we can put our plan into action."

I had no idea what "our plan" was, but "the job" was

crystal clear and unfolding in front of me. Get my parents to sign the forms: done. Eliminate them in a non-suspicious way, grab me and my inheritance, and (according to squawky wrist voice) my nose. And, frame Cliff and his dad for the crime: about to be done. Unless I did something.

"If you don't come out now," Greep sang, "I can't be responsible for what happens if this old building collapses." As if on cue, a giant plaster flower came crashing down, making a loud *boom* as it struck the floor.

I stood up, brushing aside my mom's hand. "Sit down," I said angrily. Mom and Dad stared at me for a second and then shook their heads like they were groggily waking up. But they sat down. I reached over and grabbed a wad of tissues from Mr. Kinew's desk. I closed my eyes so tightly they hurt, and I blew and blew and blew until I could blow my nose no more.

"I wish I had Fairfax the Elfling here to help me," I said. For a horrible few seconds, nothing happened. Then the tissues began to jiggle and whir, and a green fog enveloped my hand. Even though I'd wished for it, I was still so shocked that I dropped the tissues onto the floor. They continued to dance and jump, but so far, no Fairfax. I needed to stall for time.

"Jessiekins! Grab the papers," Greep howled. "And get out here NOW!"

"Coming, Garvia," I said. I stepped out of the doorway and into the chaos. Cracks were forming in the ceiling. The floor was covered with shattered glass, broken bits of chandelier and gold paint. Cliff and his dad were standing in the middle of the hall, dazed and shaking their heads.

Garvia stood in the shadows of the front doorway. "Smart girl," she said. She stole a look at the security camera on the wall above her head. She was carefully keeping herself out of sight.

I stopped. "Come and get me," I said. "Think of me as that kid in your story *Jerk and the Beanstalk*. What did the Giant do again?" Greep narrowed her eyes and growled. I held up a tissue and blew my nose. "He squashed him like a bug," I said, scrunching the tissue and throwing it back over my shoulder. "But he had to catch him first."

Greep's lips curled into an evil smile. "Easy peasy." She calmly took a chunk of debris and threw it straight up at the camera. There was a *crack* as the lens shattered. She chuckled, reached for another chunk of plaster, and began marching forward.

"Time to wipe that grin off your ugly mug," I said under my breath. Then I yelled, "Come get me, butt for brains!"

She lifted the plaster and threw it. It was coming at

me way faster than I could move. There was a flash, but it wasn't me being knocked out. A luminescent green hand was holding the plaster a hair's width in front of my nose. Fairfax the Elfling gave me a nod, then tossed the plaster aside.

Greep's smile vanished, replaced by a look of sheer panic. There was a squawk from her watch: "Is it over?" Greep didn't answer. She ran for the gaping hole where the front doors used to be. I could see the ends of a rope ladder dangling just above the sidewalk. Sirens wailed in the distance.

"Get her!" I yelled.

Fairfax rolled into a ball and flew toward Garvia. Just as Greep was about to reach the entrance, Fairfax unfurled and then tripped her. Greep did a full spin in the air and landed with a *thud* on the ground. But, catlike, she was up in a flash, punching. Fairfax dodged the first few, but then Garvia landed a clean blow on her cheek. Greep's hand sank inside, making the Elfling's head wobble, a bit like jelly.

"Ew," Greep said. She tried to extract her hand, which stayed stuck.

I ran over. Fairfax splayed the fingers on her left hand. They began to glow. It wasn't fire, like in the game, but a big, goobering mass. Greep finally extracted her hand with a loud sucking sound. Before

Fairfax could attack, Greep snatched a small vial out of her pocket and opened it. A pink vapour rose from the top. She blew it toward Fairfax's face.

"Attack!" I said. "What are you waiting for?" But Fairfax stood still, her clenched fist hovering at her side.

Greep let out a long, cold-hearted laugh. "Well, well, well. It seems my perfidious perfume works on your little minions just as well as your family and friends!" She stood up straight and slapped Fairfax across the cheek.

I felt a rising panic in my throat. "Fairfax! NO! Don't let her escape."

"It's too late," Greep said, walking backward. "But don't worry, Jessiekins. We'll meet again. And then we'll see who's the Giant and who's Jerk. And, Fairfax? Attack Jess."

Fairfax turned to face me. I stumbled back as she raised her hand. But then she winked.

"What the . . . ?" I said.

There was a loud trumpet blast from behind Greep, and then the distinct *clang* of someone being whacked with a brass instrument. Greep's eyes rolled back in her head and she fell down.

Cliff, a huge grin spreading across his face, stood in the doorway. "*Vindicta*," he said. "Victory."

The police arrived, their sirens momentarily drowned out by the loud hum of an escaping blimp. The rope ladder quickly disappeared.

"You good?" Cliff asked, gently wiping dust off his now-even-more-banged-up trumpet.

"Yeah," I said. "Thanks."

Fairfax smiled at me and blew out her hand. Then she walked over to Greep, stood on her back, and dissolved into a puddle of goo.

CHAPTER 12

NOPE-ILOGUE

The epilogue is the little bit at the end of a story that pulls together all the threads into a nice little bow. But this isn't that. It's a nope-ilogue. You see, I *thought* it was the end when the cops slapped the cuffs on Greep and hauled her away, but I was wrong. Way wrong.

Yes, Greep was taken to jail. But she was smart. The cameras never caught her image. No microphones, apparently. Just visuals, which showed Cliff and his dad acting like Han Solo on Greedo's face. In the REAL *Star Wars*. (Han shot first!)

Anyway, I'll tie up a few of the threads before telling you what happened next. But, oh boy, you won't believe what happened next!

Okay, some threads. The police recovered the vial of perfume, but it was empty. The blimp had disappeared into the clouds and gloom. Greep's watch-radio got smashed when she hit the floor, so it was just a jumble of wires and ruined microchips. Even a search of her apartment didn't turn up much. It was practically empty.

My take? Greep had been planning to escape on the blimp, with my money and possibly me, so she'd been erasing her tracks for weeks.

Mom's shop had been filled with the mind-control perfume from a canister labelled *laughing gas*. That was how Greep had kept Mom under her control all day, until it was time to grab Dad and get to the bank. Mom still had a bunch of the spiked roses with her, which was why she and Dad stayed so wonked.

Cliff had breathed in a couple lungfuls when he'd gone into the shop, which is how Greep had trapped him. But once she and Cliff headed to the bank, she'd left the door open and the gas had simply blown away. My parents and Cliff's dad snapped out of things quickly — Greep's perfume was only good for a few minutes unless it was reapplied — but it was like they had woken from a really deep sleep.

I didn't tell anyone about my superpower. I still didn't really have any evidence and Dr. F. had said to be careful. Better to keep it under wraps. Or tissues.

Mr. Kinew was the only reason the cops could even keep Greep for questioning. He suspected something was fishy about the whole paperwork stuff with Mom and Dad. And he'd been in and out of consciousness during the "robbery" and heard Greep taunting me. But he hadn't heard enough to pin everything on her. Still, that, along with my testimony, was enough to keep Cliff and his dad out of the slammer and her behind bars, for a while anyway.

My parents scratched out the forged signature and activated the account in my name, and *did* give me a cellphone for my birthday. Life is sweet. Or is it? (*Da da da daaaaaaaaaa . . .*) That's ominous music, BTW.

Let's rejoin our story a few days after Greep was arrested.

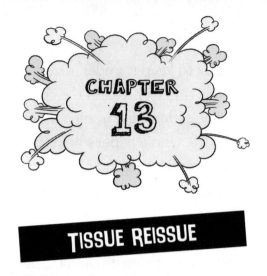

CHAPTER 13

TISSUE REISSUE

"Try making something safe, like a bouncing booger bunny," Cliff said. We were sitting in my basement, trying to figure out what made my nose run. (That's a joke, BTW.) Well, Cliff was doing his best to figure it out. I was mostly practising for *Gang of Greats*.

"Pause the battle with Mushroom Man and pay attention!" Cliff said.

"It's not a mushroom. That's his war helmet! He's a Mountain Ogre."

Cliff reached over and pressed the pause button on my controller. On the screen, Fairfax stood frozen, her sword poised to strike the fatal blow. "It's two o'clock. Time to check in."

"Ugh. Fine." I closed my eyes and blew my nose.

"I would love to have a cute widdle bunny wabbit to play with," I said, in as cloyingly sweet a voice as I could. I held the tissue in my hand and waited for any sign of movement. But it just sat there. In frustration, I crumpled it up and threw it in the garbage. Well, I threw it AT the garbage. It hit the wall and stuck.

"Remind me never to share a bowl of popcorn with you," Cliff said, shaking his head sadly. Then he took out his pen and wrote in a notebook. A new one, *not* the diary Greep had given me. The cops had that. "Okay, so it's been three hours since you made that monkey thing."

"It was a werewolf!"

"Looked like a monkey. Especially when it started chasing your cat around the room."

There was a pathetic *meow* from the ceiling. I looked up. RigaTony was dangling from the edge of the light fixture, his tail still slightly goopy from where the werewolf had tried to grab him. His claw slipped and he fell down onto the floor with a *smack*. He glared at me, hissed, and then limped away and up the stairs.

"The point is that it's been three hours and no new monsters."

"And?" I turned the game back on.

"Well, the other day you made one before school and

one after school, six hours apart. But then you made another one at the bank, only three hours after that."

"And?" I hacked at the Ogre.

"And that means there's no clear pattern for when and how your power works."

The Ogre exploded in a burst of energy. Seven, SEVEN, gold coins floated up in the air. All I had to do was jump and grab them and I'd reach Grand Master Level! I ran over and then—

"CLIFF!" I yelled. He'd shoved my shoulder just as I'd been reaching for the first coin, making my hand slip and sending Fairfax tumbling over a cliff and into the Misty Swamp. "It'll take me at least an hour to get out of here!"

Cliff pointed a finger at me. "You said there was a priority of stuff we needed to do, right?"

"We saved my parents and stopped Greep!"

"Yes. But figuring out what is causing your super-power is above practising for your video game."

"I tried making a bunny. It didn't work."

Cliff actually growled. "Just sitting here doesn't replicate the various stimuli that you were exposed to at different points during our confrontations."

"Are you speaking Latin again?"

"ARGH! Those were all English words!"

"Stimuli?"

"Well."

"Ha! Busted! I'm not a total doorknob, you know."

"The point is, we need to keep testing this power until we can figure out what's going on. Have you forgotten about the blimp?"

"The one with *Visit Dimly* on the side?"

"The *other* one!"

I smirked as I started cutting through the Viper Vines in the Marsh of Madness. Getting Cliff's goat was way too easy.

Mom called down the stairs. "Is everything okay down there?"

"Mom! Close the door!" I called back. My nose began running like crazy. Our house was yet again packed with flowers. Some supplier had to get rid of a warehouse full of tiny carnations fast. So Mom bought the lot. The shop was too small to house them, so of course, let's jam them into a house with an asthmatic teenager! I will give Mom some credit. The flowers happened to be the team colours for the Gents and Slaybirds, so she started selling boutonnieres for the big game. Ka-ching!

"We're good, Mrs. Flem," Cliff called. "Just working on some video game stuff."

"Okay. Well, there are some snacks up here if you get hungry." She closed the door.

"Snacks. Hmmm . . . Did you eat anything weird?" Cliff asked.

"You mean like anchovies and brie? That was hours before I did anything."

"I'm running out of ideas," Cliff said, closing the notebook with a frustrated slap.

I pretended to reach up and turn off a light bulb over his head. "Nap time at the genius lab."

He grabbed my hand. "Hey, wait," he said. "That's it!"

"Cliff, I need both hands to—" But it was too late. A Swamp Dragon had just reared up and blasted Fairfax with a steady stream of blue flames. She evaporated in a puff of smoke. I stared in shock as one Life Token rose from the ashes, then dissolved. The question "Resume Game?" flashed on the screen.

My controller slipped from my limp hand. My jaw went slack. I had just lost one Life Token, to a stupid Swamp Dragon. That was like a Rottweiler getting beaten up by a pigeon.

"That's funny," Cliff said, letting my hand go. "Pigeon. You really have to stop thinking out loud so much."

"So what's your big eureka moment there, Einstein?"

"Eureka was Archimedes. And before you say anything, he was Greek, not Latin . . . I mean Roman."

"Whatever. You just cost me a Life Token, Archimeathead. So this better be good."

"You said your dad has a box of old Dimly Bulbs in the garage?"

"Yeah. So?"

"I have an idea. Come on." He stood up and started walking toward the stairs. I turned off the video game, reluctantly, and was about to follow him when my phone buzzed.

"Wait," I said, scattering the empty chip bags on the TV table until I uncovered its glossy black newness. "Hello?"

A tiny voice came on. "Hello, is this Jessica Flem?"

"Maybe. Who's this?"

"Dr. Fassbinder sent me. My name is Algernon Souris, from Department C. I'm here to help you with your . . . problem."

"Problem?"

"A certain babysitter gone rogue?"

"Oh yeah. Dr. F. said he was going to send help. THREE DAYS AGO! Nice timing, Algebra."

"Algernon."

"Whatever. Where were you forty-eight hours ago when the Grim Greeper was actually trying to kill me?"

There was a pause of a few seconds. "There were some delays."

"Duh. Like what?"

He gave a tiny cough. "Well. There has been an

unexpected increase in expenditures for our department lately. Budgets are very tight."

"Boring."

"Department C could only afford a ticket on the red-eye. Sorry, let me rephrase that. I attempted to secure a place on the plane without actually paying, but was discovered. So it took me a little while to find safe transport."

"What kind of Mickey Mouse operation is this?" I said.

"You have no idea. Look, I can explain this much better in person. Can I come in?"

"Sure. Door's open. Just knock. Mom's up there."

"Oh. No need to alarm her."

"Alarm?"

But he'd hung up. I heard a scratching noise from the wall above my head. This was immediately followed by the sound of claws skidding across the kitchen floor . . . accompanied by a loud squeal.

"That would be your mom," Cliff said.

"So much for not alarming her," I said. The front door slammed and a car drove off. A second later there was a loud crash as RigaTony smashed into the basement door.

"You could have warned me about the cat!" said a voice.

Cliff and I turned to look at the stairs. At first it didn't look like anyone was there. Then we spied a small white mouse, dressed in a winter coat and a tiny tuque, skipping down the steps two at a time. He looked up at us, brushing dust off his sleeves.

"And I'll wager that your mother is off to buy some traps. If you could text her and tell her I prefer Emmenthal cheese as bait, *not peanut butter.*"

Cliff's eyes rolled back in his head and he fainted.

CHAPTER 14

STICKY SITUATION

Okay, so Cliff did not actually faint. But he did stand there stuttering and pointing at the mouse for a good ten seconds.

Algernon was not impressed. "Are you honestly telling me that I'm the *most* bizarre thing you've witnessed this week?" He unzipped his coat. He was wearing blue pants, running shoes and a white lab coat.

"Well, y– y– y– yes," Cliff sputtered.

"Highly debatable." Algernon pulled out a tiny phone and tapped the screen. "I've just accessed the Dimly Public Works Department server, and the amount of slime they've cleaned up this week suggests otherwise. Today, for example, someone reported a green wolf running around downtown. Police chased it, but it disappeared. All they found was a similar puddle."

"I thought you trapped the wolf in the garage?" I said, turning to Cliff.

"I did."

Algernon put his phone away. "The funny thing about garages is they have doors and windows. Or, your garage *did* have a window until about an hour ago. Thank goodness I arrived when I did."

"What happened?" I asked.

"I saw it escape and assumed this was one of the 'booger behemoths' Dr. Fassbinder had mentioned. So I followed it and helped it . . . fulfill its purpose."

"Which was?"

"Eating a smaller animal." He brushed more of what I now realized was dried slime off his coat before tossing it on the arm of the couch.

"Didn't that hurt?" Cliff asked.

"I leaped past the teeth before it could crunch. It swallowed me whole, allowing me to test my theory using the scientific method. And then, as I had theorized, it burped and dissolved."

"Why?" I asked.

"The monsters you . . . create . . . seem to have an 'end date,' which is the completion of whatever task you assign them when you bring them to liquefied life."

"That's why the janitor was only here for a minute," I said.

"But Fairfax stuck around until Greep was taken care of." Cliff wrote down more notes in the notebook.

"I don't know who this Fairfax you're referring to is, but if she was created to specifically stop Garvia Greep, then this makes sense. Dr. Fassbinder did mention the janitor's impermanence."

All the long words he and Cliff were using started to hurt my head. "Well, we've got it all figured out then," I said. "Nice *communicating* with you. Tell Dr. F. we've got things under control here. Bye." I waved and then started to turn on my computer again.

Algernon shook his head. "I believe not. For example, some of our other, um . . . subjects . . . have shown remarkable, and rather disturbing, limitations to their powers. Limitations that could get them killed."

Cliff gulped. "Killed?"

"He's just saying that so I'll pay attention." I said, clicking on "Resume Game." Algernon didn't bother with the controller. He walked right over and unplugged the computer. The screen blipped, then went black.

I glared at him as best I could, but I'll give the mouse credit. He had spunk. He also had a miniature telescope and he climbed up my sweatshirt and jammed it in my nose. "Can you do your mucus magic at will?"

"Hey, rude much?" I said, swatting him with my hand. I swung a little harder than I had meant to and he flew across the room. Luckily he landed in a pile of used tissues.

"I wouldn't call that lucky," Cliff said.

"Who called it lucky?" Algernon asked, standing up angrily and wiping himself down again.

"She did," Cliff said, pointing at me.

Algernon stared at Cliff for a long time, then said, "Very interesting."

Then he walked back up to me, hands on hips . . . if

mice have hips. "I repeat. Can you conjure up a 'hanky helper' at will?"

"Did you spend the entire flight here working on those bad puns?" I asked.

He just stared at me harder. "Who nose." He wiggled his whiskers, just in case I missed his latest sad attempt at humour.

"Ugh, fine. No. I can't do it at will. There seems to be some kind of time limit. But it's not regular. Cliff has some theory about how to trigger it."

Algernon climbed up Cliff's arm and sat down on his shoulder. "Do tell."

"It's just a theory," Cliff said. "But I made a joke the other day about Jess being like Aladdin and that she must have had a genie who granted wishes. But only three wishes, maybe. And then the lamp with the Splotnik bottle . . ."

Algernon nipped Cliff's earlobe. "The short version, please."

Cliff winced. "Dimly Bulbs."

"Dimly Bulbs?"

"Jess does have the power to conjure up these . . ."

"Sneeze scoundrels?"

"Seriously?" I said. "That's not even a good one."

Algernon smirked. "Go on, Cliff. I'm all ears."

"I've been keeping some notes on the various outside

factors that corresponded with Jess's episodes. And one possible link is the proximity of reidium-filled bulbs."

Algernon tapped his fingers together and paced. "Hmmm. Details?"

Cliff flipped open the notebook. "Jess busted a lamp down here the night before her birthday. Then, when Greep attacked her in the garage, there was a shattered bulb in there. Then, in the bank she was showered with stuff from the light fixtures."

"And are you sure these were all Dimly Bulb bulbs?"

Cliff shrugged. "Well, I didn't see the one down here or in the garage. But the police say the ones in the bank were original Dimly Bulbs from fifty years ago."

"Interesting. And how were you proposing to test this hypothesis on our subject?"

"*I'm right here!*" I said.

Algernon fixed me with a stare, then actually smiled. "Jessica, I feel the need to apologize."

"For showing up three days too late?"

"Ahem, no. Well, yes. But what I mean is that this is a lot to absorb for anyone, let alone a spoiled goth girl who prefers computer screens to sunlight."

"So far this is the worst apology I've ever heard," I said. "Maybe I should text Mom to get some rat poison along with the traps?"

"The others have faced some similar periods of adjustment. But, the truth is, there are dangers out there. People with evil purposes. And we must all accept that we have a role to play in stopping them."

"Whaddya mean?" Cliff said.

"Garvia Greep did not act alone. She works for a mysterious organization run by someone known only as 'The Boss.' Their intentions are global in scale. And you and the others have been given a great weapon in our fight against them."

"What intentions?"

"Simply put, they want to rule the world."

"Why not just use their mind-control stuff?" Cliff asked. "They could zap world leaders and order them around."

"We've encountered that substance once before. In a rainforest in Borneo." He closed his eyes and hung his head for a moment.

"Sure, Department C could spring for a ticket to Borneo but not Dimly," I grumped.

Algernon ignored me. "It is a chemical neurotoxin made from cats."

"Cats?" Cliff said.

"Perhaps you have heard of *Toxoplasma gondii*?"

I rolled my eyes. "Oh, please no. Not another Latin geek."

"It is a parasite that is carried by cats. Studies show that it can affect humans as well. The Boss has somehow found a way to synthesize a version that, once smelled, gives them temporary control over their subject. They call it Cat-A-Tonic."

"Oh brother," I said.

"But, it *is* temporary."

"This Boss must be a heck of a scientist," Cliff said.

Algernon frowned. "We suspect The Boss may have had help from within our own ranks."

"A traitor?"

"Many people — and yes, even mice — desire power. They may, in fact, try to recruit you to their cause. I have no doubt that if Greep had been successful in luring you into that blimp, she would have attempted to control you using the C-A-T mixture."

"She did try." I blew my nose. "She failed."

Algernon smiled. "Good. But the one thing we lack is time. Shall we test Cliff's theory before The Boss returns?"

Cliff grabbed his notebook and started walking to the stairs. "Let's go make some . . . adenoid animals."

"I'm beginning to like this boy." Algernon gave a little chuckle and grabbed his coat.

CHAPTER 15

SLIME SPREE

It turned out Dad had a few dusty cases of Dimly Bulbs stashed away in the garage. Algernon scurried up into the rafters and used a screwdriver to lift the wooden lid off one of the crates. "They are quite lovely." He held one up. It had that old-fashioned look you sometimes see in old movies. Big, with a metal wire looped inside. Dust wafted down.

"Achoo!" I sneezed, on repeat. "All right, throw it."

"NOT YET!" Cliff waved his hands frantically. "Jess needs to try making one without the light bulb first."

"Why?" I said, blowing my nose.

Algernon pulled back the bulb. "Smart lad. It's called a controlled test. If you can summon a booger beast . . ."

"Better," I said.

"Thank you." Algernon nodded. "If you can make one *without* a smashed bulb then using a bulb is a waste and tells us nothing. So give it a try."

I took another tissue and gave a big, gross blow. I tossed the tissue to the floor, which looked like it had been hit by a booger blizzard.

"Booger blizzard," Cliff chuckled.

"Can we get on with it?" Algernon yelled.

"Just try to make a rabbit or something," Cliff said.

"I could really use a fluffy bunny right now."

Nothing.

"So that's three hours and fifty-eight minutes since the ill-fated wolf incident."

"Okay, so we can assume my reidium battery is on empty. Drop the bulb now."

Algernon held out a bulb, then hesitated. "Hmmm. On second thought, no."

"Why not!" I was getting seriously impatient. The longer I sat in this stupid garage, the longer Fairfax sat trapped inside the Marsh of Madness.

"We need to know what your natural cycle is like first."

"My natural *what*?" This was starting to sound like the "talk" my mom gave me when I turned twelve.

"Time cycle. You made a wolf this morning. How long does it take to make something else, without help?" He put the bulb back in the box, disturbing bits of straw.

"Yeah. That makes sense," Cliff said, jotting down more notes.

"So you want me to sit here, for maybe another four hours, and keep making tissue wishes?" I blew my nose again. And again.

"Perhaps it won't take that long," Algernon said.

"No. I'm done. I'll be in the basement trying to save my gaming career." I turned on my heels, and stopped in shock. Cliff stood in front of the door, blocking me. *Cliff.*

"Just stay here a few more minutes," he said, his fingers gripping the edges of the door frame.

I glared at him. "Move."

He gripped the door frame even harder. "You couldn't make me if you had a TigerCat to help you."

"Listen, Toots. I wish I *had* a giant TigerCat. I'd let it eat you while I . . . wait, how do you know about TigerCats?"

Before Cliff could answer, the entire floor began to shake. I followed his eyes. The white blanket of tissues had turned into a churning tornado.

Then there was a loud rasping noise, like nails on a chalkboard, and . . .

Okay, let me pause for a second. A TigerCat is a

super-secret Easter egg hidden inside G of G's Fortress of Fantastic. Only Level Fives or higher can even try fighting it. If you can track one down, and kill it, you get an instant level boost. The problem is that they can only be killed by conjuring a MongooseSter . . . and needless to say, there aren't a lot of those scampering around the outskirts of Dimly, Manitoba.

Okay, back to the molten tornado of tissues.

The tissues became a fully formed — and apparently ferocious — TigerCat. It gnashed its teeth as it began to grow larger and larger.

"Four hours exactly!" Cliff said, looking at his watch.

I tried to slap my hand over his mouth but it was too late.

The monster jerked its head toward us, scowling. Green slobber fell from its lips. Its green talons carved angry gouges in the concrete floor. It reared, ready to lunge.

"RUN!" I yelled.

The TigerCat leaped with incredible speed. Cliff ducked just in time. The beast smashed into the door, its massive head punching a hole right through the wood. It got stuck. RigaTony gave an unholy scream from the other side.

"Your cat is going to need some serious therapy once this is all over," Cliff said.

"Shut up and help me!" I scrambled to the garage-door opener and pushed the button. The door rose. The TigerCat was almost ripping its door apart trying to get free.

"You can't let it out!" Algernon was standing on the edge of the rafter, waving frantically.

"Why not?" I yelled.

"Think of the damage that monster could do!"

"That's what I AM thinking about!" I yelled.

The garage door continued to rise. Algernon, in a move I still have trouble believing, flew through the air like a trapeze artist and landed on my head. He scrambled down my arm and pressed the button again, sending the door back down.

"Are you nuts!?" I screamed. To back me up, there was a tremendous crash as the TigerCat tore itself free. It shook its head, sending splinters of wood flying like darts.

I pushed the opener. The garage door rose.

"NO!" Algernon pushed it again. The door fell. Then he bit my hand!

"OUCH!" I yelled.

That, of course, got Mr. Kitty's attention again. It shook more slobber off its lips and bared its HUGE teeth. It lunged. We ducked. But with a swing, it ripped the door opener clear off the wall. The exposed wires spat before going silent. The TigerCat seemed confused by the plastic thing impaled on its deadly claw and just sat there for a second trying to shake it loose. We ran and cowered behind a cardboard box labelled *Old Hockey Trophies.*

"Now what?" I whispered.

"What's the final mission for this cat thing?" Algernon said.

"Jess said she was going to watch it EAT ME!" Cliff said.

Algernon seemed to consider for a moment. "That could get rid of it."

"I'M NOT LETTING IT EAT ME!" Cliff said.

"It would make things easier."

"For you and Jess!"

I felt horrible. Sure, I'd been ticked, but no one wants their best friend eaten by a carnivorous goober.

Algernon jumped on top of the box. "It's still shaking its paw. Just like a cat. Pathetic." He looked back down at us. "There must be some other way to get rid of it."

I shook my head. "You can't. Not with anything we have in here, anyway. You need a MongooseSter."

"A what?"

"It's kind of a mongoose head on top of a human body, with a lizard tail."

"Well, *make* one," Algernon said.

The TigerCat shook its paw, and the panel, along with bits of drywall, flew through the air and hit Algernon, sending him flying into my face with a *splat*. Algernon squeaked, or maybe it was Cliff. Whoever it was, the sound gave away our hiding place. I know this because the box we were hiding behind disintegrated as the TigerCat smacked it repeatedly. We bolted off in different directions. The TigerCat seemed momentarily confused and began swinging wildly.

"Now would be a good time!" Cliff said.

"I wish I had a MongooseSter," I said, running in a zigzag to avoid the claws. Nothing. "It's not working!"

There was a horrible crash as the TigerCat landed a slap on Cliff's chest and sent him flying into my dad's hockey equipment bag. He fell to the floor with a thud and lay there, moaning. The TigerCat crept toward him, licking its chops.

I reached down and grabbed a broken trophy. *Participant* was written in golden letters on the puck.

"YOU MANGY CAT!" I yelled, throwing the trophy. The marble base smacked right into the back of the beast's head. It swung around and rushed at me. I had no time to move.

"I wish I had a MongooseSter," I repeated, fully expecting them to be my last words.

Spoiler alert: they weren't.

The TigerCat knocked me to the ground. But then it stopped, slowly backing away, as if it had seen a ghost or something. I lifted my head. A tiny MongooseSter was crawling down my chest toward the TigerCat.

"Make it bigger!" Cliff yelled.

I started blowing my nose over and over, throwing the tissues at the thing. It grew and grew as it advanced on the scared cat. Then it jumped.

What followed is best described as an epic battle of strength vs. speed. The TigerCat swung its limbs wildly. The MongooseSter was able to scamper under and around them, landing blow after blow of its own. But it soon tired, and the TigerCat succeeded in landing a few heavy whacks.

Both sides took their best shots until, exhausted and injured, they retreated to opposite walls of the garage, panting for breath. For a second it looked like they were both going to surrender. But I knew better.

"The Fur-ocious Finale," I said. I'd only ever seen this on YouTube videos. Now I would see it for real.

They scuffed their claws, gnashed their teeth, and roared. Then, as if someone had yelled "GO," they sprinted toward each other at top speed, glowing with pure energy. They met in the exact middle of the garage like two bombs. The resulting explosion splattered green slime into every nook and cranny of the room. Then, silence. This was soon followed by the sound of the dripping remains of the beasts falling from the rafters.

"Best science class EVER!" Cliff said, wiping slime off his face and hair.

"How did I do that?" I said.

There was a laugh from the ceiling. I looked up. Algernon was sitting on the edge of the rafter, swinging his legs. In his hand were the remains of a smashed Dimly Bulb.

He looked at me and smiled. "Mystery solved."

CHAPTER 16

A-MUSING

I'd like to say that Cliff and I used our knowledge to keep the streets of Dimly free of crime. But, let's be honest. Dimly is the boring capital of the world, not the crime capital. The Boss was nowhere to be seen, so we did what you might expect we'd do. We had some fun.

"Fire!" I yelled. I was standing on home plate of the Dimly High softball field, staring out at Cliff on first base. He leaned back and fired a foam arrow into the air. It arced gracefully against the cloudy sky, whizzing over the tops of the nearby trees.

"I wish I had a Hazard Hawk to get the arrow," I said, blowing my nose. I flung the tissue in the direction of the arrow. Almost immediately, it transformed into the shape of the hawk, the hunting companion of every true Seventh Level Elfling. (Of *course* I'd gotten back to Level Seven. What do you think I am, an amateur?)

The hawk flew through the air and grabbed the arrow. It landed back at my feet, dropped the arrow, and then dissolved into a gloppy puddle.

There was the sound of two tiny hands clapping from the nearby bleachers. "What do you call this video game again? *Call of Snotty*?" Algernon called.

"Ha, ha," I said, then turned back to face Cliff. "Fire!"

Cliff launched another spongy arrow. I blew my nose and sent a Magma Lizard to fetch it this time. Same success, same result. Goop. We did this six more times before the power faded away.

Cliff ran over to me, slipped in the puddle, almost

surfing on the jelly-like surface, and smacked right into me. "Cool!" he said, giving me a high-five. "Booger-Girl rules!"

"Toots ain't so bad himself," I said. I have to admit it is kind of cool to have a superpower, even a gross one. Especially now that I was getting a handle on how to control it. I reached down and picked up the remains of the Dimly Bulb we'd broken.

"Maybe you shouldn't waste any more bulbs," Algernon said.

"We've only broken three this week," I said. "And how else am I supposed to test my AWESOME SUPERPOWERS?"

"It looks more like you're using it to practise strategy for your video game."

I shrugged. "Same diff. Either way, we have a pretty good idea of my battery life now."

Battery life was how Cliff referred to my "cycle." Without exposure to reidium, I could make a goober come to life every four hours. Then I had to rest to recharge.

One Dimly Bulb, however, could give me up to an hour of power, depending on how many times I used it. So far we'd capped out at about ten, although it varied by the size of the bulb and the size of the monsters I conjured.

We were running out of safe spots to practise. We'd almost gotten caught yesterday by Gary Lundborg's dad, the city maintenance guy. Okay, so maybe the Dimly swimming pool wasn't the best place to make a booger Sabre Shark. But where else was I going to find water? One little brat complains and *whammo*, the authorities show up. (I think "whammo" is Latin, BTW.)

Algernon walked over and threw a clove of garlic at me. "Time to eat," he said.

I popped it into my mouth, wincing. "Do I have to do this?"

"Reidium is a very volatile substance and you've been exposed to a lot of it lately. This is just a precaution."

I swallowed and then coughed. Cliff held his nose and handed me a small bottle of mouthwash. I swished it around and then spat on the ground.

"I think you do that just to torture me," I said.

"Torturing you is merely a bonus," Algernon said. "Now, I have some news. We have it on good authority that The Boss is intending to return."

"A job?" I asked, warily. I'd known that this was going to happen sooner or later, but I'd kind of been hoping for later. Sooner was a problem. The first G of G match was tonight and I don't care if The Boss was planning to cover Dimly in plastic wrap, I was not going to miss that.

"Probably not," Cliff said.

"Not what?" Algernon said.

"Going to cover Dimly in plastic wrap," Cliff said.

Algernon stared at him. "Very interesting," he said for like the one-hundredth annoying time.

"So what am I supposed to do, keep a lookout for a farting dirigible?" I said.

"That is definitely advisable," Algernon said, hopping down from the bleachers. "But HQ wants me to sniff around as well."

"Sniffing around is definitely not my department," I said, blowing my nose and cursing the nearby dandelions. Dimly's precious few days of spring had finally arrived.

"Just be ready to launch into action."

I saluted. "Aye, aye, Vice-Admiral Vermin."

Algernon shook his head and walked into the nearby bushes.

"Okay, so now what?" Cliff asked.

I pulled another Dimly Bulb out of my backpack. "Want to see if we can conjure up some more battle beasts?"

Cliff smiled and gave me a thumbs-up.

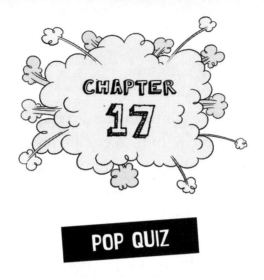

CHAPTER 17

POP QUIZ

Question number one: You know what the best thing about birthdays is? Surprises. Yes, my birthday was a week ago, but when I got home this afternoon there was an awesome surprise in the mail. Daisy had sent me an original pencil drawing she'd done. It was, I think, a bouquet of flowers. Or maybe it was a banana and a cactus. I'm not 100 percent sure.

Anyway, it was special and cool and from her. And, on the other side, she had written "Happy Birthday, Jess." I started to choke up. Then I noticed she'd added, "I hope you like this self-portrait."

Self-portrait? Okay, did not see that coming. I looked at the image again. Didn't see it going either. Who cares? I loved it. The fact that it arrived on the day of my first G of G battle seemed like a good omen, so I was going to keep it with me as a good-luck charm. The image smudged a bit where I'd put my thumb so I grabbed a sandwich bag and placed it inside.

I stole a look at the clock. Game One was going to begin in just three hours. It was time to get in some last-second practice and "get in my zone."

Question number two: You know what the worst thing about birthdays is? Surprises. So I was standing there holding the bag with the card, all weepy, when Mom and Dad walked into the kitchen, together, with their coats on.

"Um, what's up?" I said, inching closer and closer to the basement stairs. I slipped the bag into my pocket.

"We feel bad that we never got to give you a proper birthday dinner, dear," Mom said.

"We were a little distracted," Dad said.

"I refer to it as being Greeped," I said.

"Well, yes. She had us all fooled," Mom said.

"But we should talk," Dad said.

"Especially after Dr. Fassbinder updated us on some of the details about your . . . um . . . gift."

"Dr. F. told you about my phone?"

"No, dear. Your other gift." Mom pointed at my nose.
"Oh."

Dad seemed a little embarrassed. "Yeah. It's taken

us a few days to kind of think through things. We apologize for not telling you about what happened to you in the hospital. It just never seemed as real as it does now." This was about ten thousand more non-sports- or non-tax-related words than my dad had ever said to me at one time. "So we thought it might be nice to go out for a dinner and talk about stuff."

"What do you think?" Mom asked. Then they both stood there, dressed to go out, looking at me.

So parents are a little like puppy dogs. They get these big eyes and stare at you with these goofy smiles and you want to say, "Can we take a rain check? I'm busy." But you find yourself saying, "Yeah. Sure. Great. A walk. I'll get the leash."

"Okay," is what I actually said. I'm not saying my parents wagged their tails, but they looked like they might lick me, so I ran to get my coat. "But I need to be back by seven thirty, okay?" I said, heading out the door.

"Of course, dear," Mom said.

"It's not like dinner will take hours, right?" Dad said.

Two *hours* later, we were still waiting for our salads. Turns out fans had already started arriving for the big game, so everywhere was packed. We ended up at Burger Bites, Dimly's only "authentic BBQ pit." It was a pit, I'll agree with that.

"Can't we just go home and order pizza?" I begged.

Mom and Dad could tell I was getting more and more agitated, and they kept flagging down the poor server. "How long can it take to make three burgers and onion rings?" The server was so flustered that she just kept waving at us without saying a word. Every time she did, I sneezed. Cat lover.

"So tell us about your nose," Mom said.

"There's a sentence you don't hear a lot," I said. But we talked and talked as the clock ticked and ticked.

I'd started doing the math. If dinner arrived in twenty minutes I could scarf it down, jam some stupid cupcake dessert down my throat, and then usher Mom and Dad back into the car. It was only the first round, but if I missed it, it would be the last round.

"Jess. Are you okay?"

"I've got a competition tonight. I need to be home by seven forty-five at the latest."

"Isn't it better to have a real conversation with real people instead of on a computer?" Mom asked.

If your parents ever ask you that question, it's a trap. Run. But I didn't. "Reality is analog. *Gang of Greats* is digital," I said sadly.

They exchanged the look. You know, *the look*. The "Jess is spending too much time alone" look. The "maybe we should sign Jess up for yoga" look. I was so anxious about my game that I didn't sense the impending doom headed my way. But I wasn't the only one about to get whacked.

Because when Mom opened her mouth, this is what came out: "Maybe you should take Jess to the game, Jim."

Dad almost choked on his salad, and it hadn't even arrived yet. "Uh. I . . . I mean . . ."

Her eyes blazed. Poor guy. He'd never seen it coming. I have faced down Flaming Frogs that were less tenacious than my mother once she's had an idea. Nevertheless, I came bravely to Dad's aid.

"Um. That's cool," I said. "But hockey is not really my thing. You know. Sweaty dudes. Smelly pucks." There was also a very high probability that I'd have a round-two match that day.

Dad saw a glimmer of hope and joined the fight. "Yeah. You know, Bill Lundborg was sort of expecting to . . ." Dad winced. I'd seen this before and knew, without any direct evidence necessary, that he'd just had his shin kicked. Glimmer of hope? Snuffed out like a candle.

Dad turned to me. I swear I saw a lone tear slide down his cheek. "Hey, Jess. It'll be great. I'll even let you have one of those jumbo nacho Dimly Doggs." His voice was trembling.

Now, Dad loves me. That's not the issue. But taking his hockey-hating emo kid to the biggest game of his life instead of one of his beer-league buddies? Even *I* felt for him. I had to try one last attempt.

"You know, Dad . . ."

Mom jumped in before I had a chance to finish. "A father-daughter day in the fresh air. Perfect. It's settled then."

The salad arrived. It tasted like ashes in my mouth. It was a really bad salad. At least the burger, when it arrived at seven thirty-five, just tasted like burnt beef.

Dad picked at his onion rings. The fact the burger looked (and tasted) like a puck highlighted his disappointment. The rest of dinner passed without a lot more talking, but at least that made it go faster. We pulled into the driveway at five minutes to eight. I sprinted through the door and tripped over RigaTony, but got downstairs in a flash. I turned on the game.

There was a sound like a horn, and the battle was on! I leaped for my controller and sat on the couch. Fairfax was immediately attacked by a Gorg and was losing. Losing? This couldn't be Gary playing. He would have already hit the wrong button five times and fallen off a cliff.

"You're going down," beancounter3000x flashed across the screen.

I narrowed my eyes and began conjuring spells. I summoned all the animal heroes I'd been making with Cliff earlier in the day. My Hawk caught all the arrows. My Lizard bit the legs of all my enemies. Weirdly, all the panic I'd felt through dinner made me better at focusing on the game.

Finally, in an empty field, we met face to face: Elfling and Gorg. Fairfax struck first, with her patented spin-and-chop move. The Gorg launched a flaming sword that cut her arm. Fairfax fell back in pain. The Gorg attacked. I selected a Spirit Shield at the last moment and deflected the blow. The Gorg raised its arms again, the sword transforming into a SludgeHammer.

"Bad mistake," I whispered as I selected my next weapon, the Mystical Mace. I waited until the Gorg began bringing down his enormous arms, and then hit "Select." Fairfax's sword instantly transformed. It was too late for the Gorg to change tactics. His Hammer hit my Mace and exploded into a thousand pieces. The blast travelled up the Gorg's arm and soon enveloped his entire body. He twisted and writhed in pain, then exploded.

Fairfax got to her feet and walked over. Money and a Life Token rose into the air. She grabbed them, her grey-green cloak instantly turning to a shimmering silver. I had just collected the final token I needed to become a Grand Master.

"Well played," beancounter3000x typed. "Didn't think you'd have time for the Mace defence. Good luck in the next round. You'll need it."

"Who are you?" I typed. "Where have you been?"

But beancounter3000x had logged off.

I sat back against the couch and watched as Fairfax was raised into the clouds, elevated into the Hall of Greats, and given an entirely new, and super-awesome, kit of weapons.

Then the screen flashed an alert. "Congratulations, Fairfax, Grand Master Elfling. Your next challenge has been set for Saturday afternoon. Your foe will be revealed at that time. Farewell, for now."

I let out a satisfied sigh, then sat bolt upright. Saturday afternoon? ARGH! That was the same day as the stupid hockey game.

CHAPTER 18

STUPID HOCKEY GAME, MEET EXCELLENT PLAN

It was no use trying to get out of the game by pretending to be sick. I was always sick.

"Doomed," I said.

Cliff and I were sitting on my front step. He was happily polishing his trumpet. He'd improved so much Miss T. said he could be in the band for the big game. My computer sat, powered down and ignored, in the basement below. I didn't even have the energy or motivation to practise. Or to keep my superpowers sharp. Not that we'd heard a peep from Algernon in days.

"I think he squeaks, not peeps," Cliff said.

"Whatever. Nothing can stop the A-puck-alypse. The end of my G of G career. Killed by hockey."

And then Cliff came up with the solution: "Booger-Girl!"

"That's my nickname, don't wear it out," I mumbled.

"No. I mean *make* a Booger-Girl."

"Why?"

"Conjure a Jess who can play for you while you're at the hockey game."

I sat up and slapped him on the back. "Cliff, you're a genius!"

"I know. Think about it. You can have a great time with your dad, wave to me during the intermission, buy me a Dimly Dogg, and watch the biggest game in the world. You might even get on TV around the world!"

"Genius credentials revoked," I said with a frown.

"Why? It's a perfect plan."

"I'm not going to any stupid hockey game." I wiggled my eyebrows. "But, I won't have to!"

"Why not?"

"Duh. I'll conjure up a Jelly Jess to go with my dad, and *I'll* stay here."

"Won't your dad start to suspect something's up?"

"We'll slap my clothes on Jess 2.0. Dad will be so preoccupied with the game he won't even notice." Cliff looked skeptical. "I'll get her to keep a tissue in front of her nose the whole time. Nothing suspicious there." I blew my nose and threw the tissue on the ground.

Cliff stared at the tissue. "I like that one," he said. "Looks like a white truffle." He snapped a photo, then pulled a bag out of his backpack and stuck the tissue inside. "Exhibit 375b. Truffle."

I wasn't really paying attention. I was working out the details of my super-excellent plan.

The morning of the big game arrived. Dad was doing his best to act cheerful, but he was moping around the house. Even his Winterpeg Gents face paint seemed a sadder shade of blue. I tried the "I have a cold" gambit but, as expected, Dr. Mom didn't bite. "You just need a few hours of sunlight and fresh air," she said.

That was okay. The sickness ploy was stage one of my Excellent Plan. I bundled myself up in a thick scarf, big winter coat and heavy tuque. Then, just an hour before it was time to leave, stage two. Cliff showed up. I'd convinced him to ride to the game with "us," and he'd agreed to keep talking to Dad in the car, further distracting Dad from Fake Jess.

"Okay, Jess," Dad said. "Let's go."

"Yay!" I said. "Oh, wait. I just left something downstairs. We'll be right back." I grabbed Cliff's hand.

"Still incredibly skeptical," Cliff said.

Stage three: I blew my nose and threw the tissue onto the pile I'd been prepping all week. "I wish I had a Jess to go to the hockey game with my dad," I said.

YES! The pile instantly began to swirl. Within seconds a goobery green version of me stood in my basement. I took off my coat, scarf and tuque and wrapped up Fake Jess as tightly as I could. Then I handed her a box of tissues. "Blow your nose *as much as possible*," I said.

Fake Jess nodded and held a tissue up to her nose. I stepped back and took a good look. "Perfect," I said. "You can barely see any green at all." I looked at Cliff. "If Dad suspects anything, just tell him you and I were doing a surprise face painting down here, and it didn't go great."

"C'mon, Jess!" Dad called down the stairs.

"Coming," I said. Then I ducked down behind the couch.

Cliff took Jess's hand and turned to head upstairs. "I didn't think it was possible to be MORE skeptical. I was wrong."

"Don't worry so much. This plan is excellent," I whispered at him.

And within minutes my Excellent Plan began to unravel, thanks to Stupid Reality.

CHAPTER 19

EXCELLENT PLAN, MEET STUPID REALITY

Now, I'm not completely deluded. I figured there was a possibility that Dad would discover Fake Jess was a fake, and that the longer she sat with him the bigger the chances. So I had a Plan B. I'd wrap up the G of G match as quickly as I could, then head to the hockey game, sneak inside, and get rid of Fake Jess before Dad suspected anything was fishy.

Not long after Dad left, Mom got into her car and drove away. She had a few boutonnieres left and had been toying with the idea of selling them outside the game. So she was obviously off to make a little extra cash. "Yes!" I said. Luck was on my side.

I was alone now, so I turned on the lights and the computer. I took Daisy's card out of the protective bag and leaned it against the computer screen for good luck. Then I waited.

At two o'clock everything exploded, and I'm not just talking about the video game. That was going well. I was up pretty quickly on a gamer named Yawesome Yeti who, in fact, had a Yeti Warrior as his avatar. *Very creative*, I thought sarcastically.

But halfway through our battle, my phone buzzed. I ignored it. It buzzed again. And again. It buzzed so much it fell off the table and smacked my hand. I slipped. Fairfax's shield changed into a large coconut and the Yeti almost lopped her arm off. The phone kept buzzing. It was hard to concentrate.

I took a time out. We were only allowed three, so I wasn't happy. It was Cliff. I hit speakerphone.

"What?" I said.

"Jess. It's a disaster, a total disaster. You've got to get here." He seemed to be whispering into the phone. I could barely hear him over the crowd.

"I can't. I'm playing *right now*." My finger hesitated over *end call*.

"Don't press that!"

"What could be so wrong?" The time out was counting down from thirty.

"What did you ask for?"

I thought back. "A fake Jess to go to the game with Dad." Twenty seconds left.

"ARGH!"

"What?"

"Fake Jess did *go* to the game with your dad. Then as soon as we all lined up for the security check, *gloop*."

"Oh no." I smacked my forehead. Ten seconds.

"Yeah. Luckily I saw it happen and grabbed the tuque and scarf while your dad was fumbling for the tickets. He grabbed my hand. I did my best Jess voice, blew my nose, and now he thinks I'm you."

The game resumed. I muted the sound but began slashing at the Yeti with my Axe of Wonder.

"Good thinking, Toots! I'm proud of you."

"No, you don't get it. I'm TRAPPED IN THE STANDS."

"Well, enjoy the game," I said.

"But the band nee—"

I hung up and resumed my fighting. Within seconds, I had the Yeti on the run. Then my stupid phone started buzzing again. I hit answer.

"Cliff, I don't have time for—"

"Cliff?" said a squeaky voice. It was Algernon. "Jess, where are you?"

"I'm *trying* to be in Greatlandia, fighting a Yeti, but I keep getting interrupted."

"But . . ." I ended the call. The phone buzzed again. I ignored it. *Annoying lab rat.* The battle continued.

Next thing I knew, Yawesome Yeti took a time out. A message popped up from AsseomeDud27: "Jess. BUMP mgt ber hoodinggg yarll wy. LOK FORRT IT!"

I messaged back, "BUMP?" But Gary didn't respond. And what the heck did "lok forrt it" mean?

Then Cliff called again. "GET HERE NOW!" he said, as I heard the last strains of the anthem ringing out behind him. I hung up.

Algernon called just as the time out was ending. "JESSICA FLEM. DO NOT HANG UP!" I hung up.

Time out over, and the Yeti had gained ten Power Points. How was that possible? AH! He'd fought a side battle on his phone during the time out to get extra stuff. "Should call yourself Cheating Weasel," I hissed.

But I was a Grand Master. I didn't need to cheat. Also, to be honest, every time I reached for my phone, it buzzed with more calls. Cliff. Algernon. Cliff. Cliff. Algernon. Algernon.

Then the police called the home phone. Uh-oh. I paused the game for my second time out and stretched for the closest handset. "Um, yes?"

"Is this Mrs. Flem?" she said.

I made my voice go slightly lower. "Yes. Yes it is. How can I help you, officer?"

"We have some strange news." The hairs on my neck stood up. Whatever the police officer said next was guaranteed to be bad. It was. "Mr. Kinew from the bank has recanted his statement. We had no choice but to let Garvia Greep go."

I shivered. "Wait. How did Mr. Kinew sound when he recanted his statement?"

"Funny you mention that. He sounded a little bit like a robot. But he said he was just tired. He had this weird smell too, like cat pee and—"

"Burnt rubber?"

"Yeah. But I'm a cop, not a perfume expert. Anyway, we're keeping an eye on her. She's not near your home or anything, or the bank. Appears she scored a ticket to the big game. She's at the stadium. Just thought you'd want to know." She hung up.

My time out had ended. Fairfax was being smashed to a pulp by the Yeti and I hadn't even noticed. I quickly picked up the controller and began fighting back, my Energy Points dipping precariously low.

But my head was only half on the game now. The other half was racing to connect all the info that was getting thrown at me. Someone had gotten to Mr. K. They wanted Greep sprung, now, today. And she was heading to the game. The game where my dad was sitting with my best friend. The game where Mom was standing outside selling flowers. The game the world was going to be watching. The game where thousands of people were about to be attacked. But how? Why?

Wait. What if Gary had been trying to type "BLIMP might be heading your way" instead of "BUMP mgt ber hoodinggg yarll wy"? The blimp. Cat pee. Burnt rubber. The Boss was back, and the number-one stenchman, Greep, was free. I didn't know what they had planned, but I knew I had to do something. That's why Algernon had been calling me. It was up to Booger-Girl to save the day.

It hurts to even say this, but suddenly Fairfax didn't matter so much. I needed to be a REAL hero. I stood up. I took my final time out. Okay, Fairfax still mattered a little. I blew my nose and looked at the tissue.

"I wish there was another Jess here to play — no, to WIN — this game for me."

All of a sudden, the tissue began to churn. Within seconds, a miniature version of me jumped out and ran to the controller. She was tiny, but danced from button to button like a ballet superstar — faster than my thumbs ever could. I grabbed Daisy's card and put it back inside the bag. I needed all the good omens I could get.

The time out ended but I didn't stay to watch. I sprinted up the stairs, into the garage, and onto my bike. As the garage door opened, I sent a text to Cliff and Algernon: "BoogrGrl to the rescue!"

BOOGRGRL TO THE RESCUE?

The cheering broke like waves the closer I got to the stadium. My phone was buzzing, but I couldn't stop to look at it now. I had wasted too much time on my video game obsession and now everyone was at risk. Well, "wasted" isn't exactly the right word. I still hoped Jess would beat that stupid Yeti.

But how was I going to sneak inside the stadium? My original plan was to somehow get Cliff to let me in through the stage-performers' door. Of course, he was trapped playing me . . . unless he was smart enough to try dodging out? Hmmmm. Nah, better not rely on that.

Mom was probably still camped in front of the main entrance, so that was a no-sneak zone. All the gates had security guards. All the security guards wanted to see tickets. All I had was a hoodie stuffed with tissues. Some of them clean.

I spied the school band's bus parked near the stadium's backstage entrance, and Miss Terioso frantically searching inside for something. I screeched to a halt and jumped off my bike.

"Hey, Miss T.," I called through the open window.

She ran over. "Where is my trumpet player?"

"I think I know where he is," I said. "If you can get me into the stadium, I'll go get him for you." I flashed my sweetest smile.

She considered for a moment. "C'mon," she whispered, almost as if she were a spy or something. That's the funny thing about adults. They always tell you not to do anything "wrong," but *they* are itching to do that stuff all the time. She led me up to the closest security guard, who was staring intently at a big screen showing the game. It was tied 0–0. "This is Jess. She forgot her accreditation. But she's a BIG part of the band."

"Uh-huh." The security guard seemed more concerned with what was happening in the game. She took one quick glance at me, judged me a weirdo but probably not a risk, looked at Miss T.'s pass, and waved us through. We passed through a big black curtain and into the stadium. I realized with a jolt that I had no idea where my dad's seats were.

Miss T. knelt down and put her hands on my shoulders. "Jess, if he's not here in twenty minutes, we're ruined."

"I'm on it." She hurried to wherever the band was warming up and I pulled out my phone. Sure enough, I'd gotten so many calls my voicemail was full.

Didn't matter. I texted Cliff. "I M Here. Where R U?"

There was an agonizingly long wait, then finally, "Section 115, outside women's washroom. FESTINATE." I assumed that meant "hurry." I was near section 125. I sprinted to my right, rushing through people, passing snack bars and souvenir stands as the numbers fell. There was a loud horn from the stands as the first period ended.

I turned a corner and skidded to a stop. Cliff was there, but Garvia Greep was too! She'd grabbed him by the scarf and was leading him away. I was about to charge, when my dad came out of the vomitorium.

(Side note. I know it sounds like my dad was puking somewhere, but no! *Vomitorium* is the one Latin word Cliff taught me that I like. It means the hallways in big stadiums. They "vomit" or spit out the fans. Isn't that cool?)

Anyway, Dad came sprinting out of the *vomitorium*

(so cool!) and onto the walkway, looking frantically down both directions of the hallway.

"Garvia?" he bellowed. "GET AWAY FROM MY DAUGHTER!" He ran toward them, fists clenched, growling furiously. I felt a swell of pride, and even choked up a bit. Here's the weird thing. Greep didn't seem worried. She just pulled some doohickey out of her pocket. It had a big red button.

Red buttons are *never* good. She pressed it. All around me, people stopped in their tracks, Dad included. Their boutonnieres had begun spraying small puffs of pink gas, right into their faces. Dad, the loving husband, was actually wearing five. Poor sap. He was so stunned by the gas, he fell down face first onto the floor, luckily into an extra-large cheese nacho platter that someone had just dropped. The entire arena had gone silent.

I'm pretty sure that if I could smell I would have picked up the aroma of cat pee and burnt rubber. Mom's secret flower supplier? It had been Greep and The Boss! They had sabotaged my mom, again, and knocked out my dad, again. And now they had Cliff under their spell, again.

"Booger-Girl to the rescue," I hissed. I blew my nose and stepped out into the middle of the hallway. "Garvia Greep, you stupid creep!" I yelled. She stopped and turned to face me. She looked from Cliff to me and back again, confused. I threw the tissue at her.

"I wish I had a Fire Dragon to teach Greep a lesson."

Nothing happened. The tissue hit the floor, bounced twice, and then stopped. Making two Jesses had drained my powers! Greep stared at the immobile tissue and then looked back at me. She sneered. "Sinus trouble, Jessiekins? Awww. Too bad."

She shoved Cliff aside and marched over to me. She was surprisingly fast, and I was so shocked I didn't move. She grabbed me by the arm. My phone skidded across the floor toward Cliff, who just lay there like he'd been knocked out.

Greep lifted her wrist and spoke into her watch. "Target acquired. On our way." Her grip was iron tight. I struggled but couldn't break it. "Nice try dressing up your buddy in your sloppy clothes. He's asleep now, like everyone else."

I looked back. No, he wasn't! Cliff had wrapped the scarf so tightly around his face that it had acted like a gas mask. He was faking it!

Cliff, get up, I thought.

Cliff's eyes locked on mine and he nodded. Wait . . . I definitely hadn't said that out loud. It hit me like a brick in the face. What Algernon kept finding so "very interesting" about Cliff. I hadn't been *thinking* out loud all those times. Cliff could hear my thoughts. How was that possible?

Greep marched me toward the edge of the walkway. I heard a whirring noise, a few loud bangs, and saw the sooty rungs of a rope ladder slap against the concrete.

Chompo bars, I thought. *Chompo bars. CHOMPO BARS!*

Cliff grabbed my phone. I hoped he understood. Greep reached for the lowest rung, her grip on my arm like a vice. In just a few seconds we'd be gone.

Cliff walked over, robotically, like he had back at the bank. "Oh great Garvia Greep," he said, laying it on a bit too thick, I thought. "The Boss says the communicator on board is broken. You are to take this call."

Greep looked skeptical, but then she muttered something about "cheap audio equipment," and grabbed the phone. She held it up to her ear. "Yes, Boss, what is it?" Instantly her eyes glazed over. She nodded. Her hand let go of the ladder, and me. "Chompo," she said. "Chompo." She walked toward the snack bar.

Cliff had understood! The Chompo bar ad had kept popping up on my game and it took Cliff about two seconds to find it.

"You rock, Toots," I said.

"Thanks," he said. "But now what?"

Before we could move, Greep let out a ferocious scream and threw the phone down, smashing it to bits.

"Hey! That was my birthday present!" I yelled.

She grabbed her head like she'd just eaten a carton of freezing-cold ice cream and fell to her knees.

"RUN," I said. Cliff and I sprinted into the jam-packed bowl of Dimly Field. I turned, but Greep wasn't chasing us. Without looking, I smashed into Cliff, who had stopped cold.

"Whoa," he said in a low whisper.

It's hard to describe the scene properly. Everyone — the crowd, the sideline reporters, the players — was standing stock-still, or slumped over their seats, like statues. The first period had ended, but nothing moved.

A scratchy voice boomed from the sky: "People of Dimly. You will awake soon and remember nothing. The game will resume as if nothing had happened. NOTHING. Got it?" Like a rotten melon, the Badyear Blimp appeared over the side of the stadium, belching smoke and gas.

"We gotta move!" I said.

Cliff's phone rang as we scurried down the steps two at a time. It was Algernon. Cliff handed it to me. "Jess, I don't have time to explain." He sounded out of breath, like he was running. "The Boss's henchcats are roaming through every house, stealing light bulbs and Splotnik bottles."

"Splotnik bottles?"

"I ran some tests. The paint in the label contains reidium."

"Algernon, what's going on?"

"They are stealing every source of reidium they can find. Who knows what they will try."

I looked around at the frozen fans. "Is it possible they plan to zap a whole town full of hockey fans?" I asked, with a growing sense of terror.

"That would appear to be a distinct possibility. The cats are being controlled by some sort of tracking device. I've traced the signal back to Dimly Field."

"The blimp," I said.

"It's back? I'll try to get there to help," he said.

"Yeah. See you in three days. If Department C can spring for the cab fare."

"This is no time for sarcasm," Algernon said. Then there was a loud, cat-like screech and the phone went dead.

"Algernon!" I called, but it was no use. I hung up the phone and handed it back to Cliff.

"Booger-Girl. You know what we need to do, right?"

I gazed at the blimp. "Yeah. But I'm not happy about it."

"If The Boss's crew escapes with all that reidium, there's no telling what they will try to do with it."

The blimp was now hovering over centre ice. "What are they waiting for?" I asked.

The answer came in a rush of fur and fury. We felt it in our feet first, as a low rumble. Then the entire stadium began to vibrate.

"What the heck?" we both said.

A tidal wave of cats swept through the doors and onto the rink. Each was wearing a metallic-looking backpack weighed down by whatever was inside. Two particularly large cats smashed right into the legs of the Barfalo goalie and knocked him down.

"Look!" Cliff said, pointing to centre ice. Greep hadn't chased us because she had another job to do.

She was lifting the cats, one by one, into some basket that raised them up and into the waiting blimp.

It was now or never. I turned to Cliff. "I can't ask you to come with me, Toots."

"Just try keeping your sidekick—"

"Comic relief."

"Whatever. Just try keeping me down here. We're in this together." Our eyes locked for an awkward moment. "You gonna puke again?" Cliff asked. I slugged him on the arm and we ran toward the blimp.

Greep was lifting the last cat into the basket. She grabbed the rope ladder and said something into her watch. She looked at us and gave a wave. "So long, suckers!" Then up she climbed. The propeller on the blimp spat and whirred. We slid on the ice, but arrived just as the blimp began to rise up.

"Jump!" I yelled.

Cliff and I leaped at the same time and almost smashed into each other, but we wrapped our hands around the coarse rope and held on.

CHAPTER 21

SOONER OR LADDER

I looked up. Greep was disappearing into the belly of the blimp, which was spewing yet more smoke and gas. We rose slowly. Down below, the people in the crowd remained as still as statues. They'd wake up soon and would have no idea what had just happened.

Poor Dad, I thought. He was about to find me gone.

"Poor Miss T.," Cliff said. "She'll be looking for a trumpet player who'll never arrive."

We scrambled up the last few rungs of the ladder. I yanked the door open and we spilled onto the bridge. It was completely empty. No Greep. No cats. The steering wheel turned but no one was there.

I walked toward the wheel. "Let's turn this junky

balloon around," I said. Before I could say another word, something smacked me in the face. I fell backward into Cliff's arms. "What the—?"

Then something swept our feet out from under us and we flipped onto our backs.

"Who's there?" I yelled, scrambling to get up.

"And where?" Cliff added.

The first response was a low, hollow laugh. "I've waited a long time for this moment, Jessica." An invisible hand grabbed my cheeks and shook my head. "Ever since you were a baby I knew you would eventually show your powers. Powers that I will soon employ to rule the world!"

Baby? "Nurse Nussbaum!" I said. "But you died!"

Nussbaum cackled. "Did I?"

I swung my fists wildly, hitting nothing. "I beat you at the bank," I said. "And I can kick your butt in a blimp too."

"Not this time." Nussbaum laughed, with a hacking cough. "That loss, as you call it, was a shock. I won't deny it. But we learned so much, so very, very much."

"What do you mean?" Cliff said.

"We'd been thinking so small. Kidnap you. Steal your money. But once we saw what you were capable of! What reidium had done, how it had transformed you into something beautiful, strange and deadly."

"And a little gross," Cliff mumbled.

"Then I knew we had to return for you."

"You knocked out a whole stadium full of people just to trap me?"

"Seems a little over the top," Cliff said.

Nussbaum laughed with a rasping laugh, now from somewhere to our left. "You two lack vision. Just like that pathetic Fassbinder. He never saw the possibilities of what reidium could do, and now he's surrounded by a bunch of stupid cheese-eating rodents and a government job. I've got booger plans."

Cliff started laughing.

"Why are you laughing, you cretin?"

"You said 'booger plans'!" Cliff was laughing so hard he had to grab his ribs.

"I certainly did not," Nussbaum said.

Cliff just nodded, sputtering out, "Yes, you did."

I tried to take advantage of the distraction to run for the steering wheel, but Nussbaum tripped me with an invisible foot. Then she was on me, twisting my ear. "I'll show you how much *bigger* my plans are," she said. She soon had Cliff by his ear as well. She dragged us through the bridge and into the hull of the blimp. With no one at the helm, it rose and fell like a bird with one wing. A constipated bird with one wing. A constipated bird with one wing and carrying a coconut in its beak. She threw us to the floor. "Look."

I looked. The blimp was jammed from floor to ceiling with crates of Dimly Bulbs and Splotnik bottles, hundreds of barrels with *Danger: Toxic* written on them in fluorescent paint. There was even a crate of art supplies labelled *Dimly Pencil Company*. Cats, hundreds of them, sat on the rusted iron girders, licking their paws.

Greep sat on one of the barrels, smirking. "You were right, Boss. She was stupid enough to follow me up here. I owe you a thousand bucks. Once I have control of Jess's account, I'll send it right over."

"You were the worst babysitter ever," I said.

Nussbaum kicked me. "The entire stockpile of Dimly's reidium is now in this blimp. Soon I will control the world supply, and then no one can stop me!"

"And?"

"And the grovelling idiots of the world will bow down to me."

"I will stop you," I said.

"Me too," Cliff said.

Cliff recoiled as Nussbaum slapped him on the cheek. "YOU are nothing but comic relief," she said.

"Told you," I said. Cliff frowned.

"Soon the entire population of Dimly will be part of my *army*."

"What army?" I clenched my fists. "You said the crowd would wake up and remember nothing."

"That's because I wanted you to think we were leaving. Instead you've left all those people down there alone. I've seen what a little reidium can do for you, and can't do. Garvia tells me you were unable to summon even a one-tissue gob goblin."

"I'll have to remember that one," I said to Cliff. He nodded.

"But if you'd been exposed to the amount of reidium I'm about to drop, there's no telling what you could do."

"You wouldn't dare," I hissed.

"Oh, but I will. In five minutes intermission will be over. I will release a cloud of reidium over Dimly Field. A tenth of what I have on board will be enough. The world will watch in horror and amazement as I transform these slack-jawed hosers into a mutant army."

"You'll kill them!" Cliff yelled.

Nussbaum snorted. "Are you kidding me? The amount of garlic in the Squid Tortillas alone will mediate the effects."

"Yeah, like you're an expert," I scoffed.

Nussbaum grabbed my cheeks again. "I have performed numerous experiments since my unfortunate . . . accident. Using my newly refined Cat-A-Tonic, I will control them, and whatever powers they develop. If some of them do die, it will be a small price to pay."

If she was holding my cheeks, she was close. I kicked out in the direction of her laughter and guessed right. There was a smash as Nussbaum the Invisible fell to the ground. "I wish I had a Troll to rip you apart!" I said, but nothing happened.

I felt a steel grip on my neck and began to gag. Greep had come to her boss's rescue and was holding Cliff and me by the scruff of our necks. "You fool. The reidium here is surrounded by a lead screen. You are powerless, just like the lambs in *Little Bo Greep*."

"That was your worst book," I croaked. "And that's saying a lot." She choked me even harder.

"Enough!" Nussbaum yelled. "Garvia, throw them in the containment cage!"

"Gladly." Greep marched us over a metal gangplank and threw us into a large, windowless metal box.

"You'll be a helpful weapon, Jessiekins, when the time comes," she said, before closing the door. "If you're really good, I'll read you a bedtime story tonight." She slammed the door. Cliff and I threw ourselves against it, but it was no use. We were trapped.

All the cat hair was making my nose run overtime. I had one unused tissue left. "Here's a few more," Cliff said, handing me some scrunched-up ones.

"Thanks, Toots." I blew my nose and then sat down against the wall, my head between my knees, utterly defeated. I'd been tricked. Tricked into getting myself captured. Tricked into getting my best friend captured. Tricked into letting my parents and my town get irreidiated by my old nurse and my horrible babysitter. And who knew if Jess was still competing in *Gang of Greats*!

A part of the wall slid sideways, revealing a TV screen. The hockey game was set to resume. Nussbaum's voice came over a speaker, filling our cell. "We now return you to your regularly scheduled programming, already in progress."

The TV announcer seemed to be waking up from a dream. "Welcome back to Dimly Field, everyone." He yawned. "Well, I'm not quite sure what's going on, but we seem to have had some technical difficulties. The players haven't even budged! Let's go to Belinda down rinkside."

"Well, Frank, I guess the players were having so much fun they decided to stay on the ice. One of the benefits of SynthetICE is that it doesn't need resurfacing. They seem ready to resume playing, and the crowd seems to be waking up too. This guy in particular seems totally stoked!"

A camera panned toward the crowd. My father emerged from the archway, his face now a mixture of Winterpeg blue and fake-nacho-cheese orange. He was frantically looking around for me, utterly unaware that he would soon join me in Section M, for mutant.

"Hey, Belinda, what's that up there?" the announcer asked excitedly. The camera panned to the sky, Nussbaum's blimp barely discernible against the gathering clouds. "Is that a flying poop emoji?" Even through the metal door, I heard Nussbaum scream something I won't repeat here.

"Actually, Frank, I think that's a second blimp. Maybe Dimly Sewage has signed on as a last-minute sponsor?"

"*Second* blimp," Cliff said. "Hey, yeah. Where is the other one?"

I shrugged.

Nussbaum's voice came back on. "You might want to watch, Jess. Things are about to get very interest—" She didn't finish.

"LOOK!" Cliff said, pointing at the screen. The other blimp, the real one, was here. And it was heading straight for us. Just like a TigerCat and a MongooseSter, the two blimps were on a Fur-ocious Finale collision course.

"Yay!" Cliff yelled.

"Wait," I said. "If they smash into us, we'll crash right into the field!"

"BOOO!" Cliff yelled.

The blimps drew closer. We began to sway as Nussbaum took evasive action. But looking at the screen it was obvious: we were doomed.

CHAPTER 22

DOOM FOR TWO

I stared at the useless tissues scattered on the floor and racked my brain. On the TV, the blimps drew ever closer. I thought back to my day, my last day on Earth, the scenes coming back to me in screenshots. My brain stopped on the image of Dimly Pencils.

"Dimly Pencils?" Cliff said, reading my thoughts.

I pulled Daisy's card out of my pocket. "When I was home, I was able to make a tiny version of me. It didn't even occur to me then because I was so panicked, but I shouldn't have been able to. Except I had this next to my computer."

I opened the bag. "It must contain some small level of reidium." I took a big sniff and then blew my nose. "I wish I had a Gorg to smash us out of this room."

The tissue lurched and spun in the air, sucking the remaining tissues into its vortex.

"It worked!" Cliff said. Sort of. The Gorg was only about half the size of Algernon. "Not that much reidium in the pencil, apparently," Cliff said.

But Gorgs are strong. He started ripping and tearing at the door. Bit by bit, he began to form a tiny Gorg-sized hole in the metal. It would never be big enough for Cliff and me to get through.

"This is incredible!" Belinda was saying on the TV. "The crowd has completely forgotten about the game, their eyes now glued to the sky!" Our blimp had barely moved, swinging droopily in the air. The other blimp was only a minute or so away.

With one final blast, the Gorg burst through the door. "Well, that's disappointing," Cliff said, sticking his finger through the hole. But then there was a *click* and the door swung open. I rushed outside. Greep had been standing guard a couple of metres away and with rage in her eyes, she ran at me.

The Gorg was hanging from the door handle. He gave me a salute, jumped in front of Greep, and dissolved into a puddle of goop. Greep slipped on the Gorg droppings like a clown on a banana peel and flew through the air. She landed with a thud, out cold.

"Well, that was easy," Cliff said.

"Yeah, but we could see Greep."

"True enough."

"Okay, Toots. Let's get to the bridge."

I reached for Daisy's card. "I'll make another Gorg to help us," I said. But just then there was a loud ripping sound from above us. The stress of our sudden turn had loosened the seams on one of the patches. A cold breeze swept in, snatched the card from my hands, and carried it off into the sky.

"NO!" We dipped suddenly. Cats were flying through the sudden weightlessness.

"Ouch!" Cliff yelled, as cat after cat smacked into him. The blimp rose again, sending all of us crashing to the floor. I don't need to tell you how stuffed my nose was now. So I won't.

"Hurry. We don't have much time," Cliff said.

Nice to know you'll be able to steer this thing, I thought, inching forward.

"Whaddya mean?"

"Well, you are CAPTAIN OBVIOUS!"

We reached the back door of the bridge. The blimp was still bobbing and weaving ominously. The only evidence that Nussbaum was still there was the frantic turning of the steering wheel as she attempted to escape the inevitable collision.

"I'm going in," I said. I slammed the door open and

ran straight at the steering wheel. I was stopped by Nussbaum's invisible butt.

"You little fool!" she yelled. An invisible hand struck me and I fell backward. The steering wheel began to spin wildly on its own and the entire blimp lurched. She was coming for me. I stood up. The other blimp came into view outside the side window. It was close enough that I could see into the bridge. The wheel was being turned by a tiny mouse wearing a lab coat and blue pants.

"ALGERNON!"

I ran for the window but was tackled from behind. *Cliff*, I thought, as Nussbaum mushed my face into the floor. *Make Algernon see you.*

Cliff reached the window and waved frantically, yelling, "Algernon! EVASIVE ACTION."

He looked back. "It's no good! We're too close!"

There was a horrible screech as the blimps smashed into each other. But we didn't crash. At the last second, Algernon had swerved. We'd collided, but not head-on. Instead, his side hit ours, like balloon bumper cars. We stayed rubbing against each other for what seemed like an eternity, the cloth making horrible scraping noises, more seams bursting. Then we separated, our blimp spinning and diving out of control.

"You're ruining everything!" Nussbaum cried.

"*You* did that, years ago!" I yelled. I ran for the wheel and directed us away from the field. Within seconds her invisible hands fought mine for control.

"I WILL HAVE MY ARMY!"

"You're insane!" The entire downtown of Dimly now filled the front window, growing closer and closer, and bigger and bigger. This was not good. "I wish I had a pilot!" I said. Nothing.

Nussbaum tried to pry my fingers from the wheel.

I kicked out, landing a few blows on her leg. It bought me enough time to straighten us out. But straight wasn't exactly the best thing, because we were heading *straight* for a line of row houses.

"Hey! That's *my* house!" Cliff yelled, pointing.

"A little help here!" I yelled over my shoulder.

"Oh. Yeah," Cliff said. He ran up behind and took a swing at Nussbaum. Of course, not being able to see her, he missed and hit me instead. I fell sideways, lurching the wheel as I fell.

"Nice job, comic relief!" I said.

"Sorry."

"We're going to crash!" Nussbaum yelled. The wheel yanked backward, but it was too late. The cockpit of the blimp smashed right into the second floor of Cliff's house. Window met window, the glass shattering. The blimp tilted up as the engine tried to keep it moving forward. Cliff and I were thrown out of the blimp and onto his bedroom floor. The blimp jerked and shuddered as Nussbaum jammed it into reverse. The engines whined horribly.

"We've got to stop her," I said. "She's going to get away."

"She'll head back to Dimly Field!" Cliff said.

There was a flash as a blast of energy flew past me, smashing into Cliff's bedroom wall. Greep was standing next to the wheel, a bump the size of a baseball on her head. She aimed her blaster and fired. The bolt just missed Cliff's head and hit his display cabinet.

"My collection!" he yelped. Hundreds of plastic-wrapped tissues fell to the ground, many of them now on fire. Cliff tried to stomp out the flames. I gritted my teeth. There had to be some way to fight back!

I climbed onto the windowsill but was thrown back by a huge explosion. The cockpit filled with smoke. Greep stuck her head out of the window, hacking and coughing. The engines gave an even louder hack, then stopped whirring. The rear end of the blimp sank like a stone, so suddenly that Greep fell and disappeared.

"What just happened?" Cliff said.

I pointed at the bridge. Algernon had jumped on top of the steering wheel. He was holding up what seemed to be a can of spray paint. He propped it on the wheel and pushed the button.

A cloud of red paint filled the air. Nussbaum began to take visible form as he covered her in paint. She swung at Algernon and caught him full on the chest. He flew toward us. I reached out and caught him in mid-air. I gently laid him on the floor, his arms still wrapped around the paint can.

"Algernon, I am *not* doing mouth-to-mouse on

you," I said. Algernon smiled. Then he held up his hand and sprayed me right in the chest.

"What the heck are you doing?" I screamed. He turned the can around so I could see the label. *Dimly Dye: Developers of Dynamite Decorative Daubs.*

"Reidium," I whispered, feeling the power surge through me.

"Go for it, Booger-Girl," Algernon croaked. Then his arm fell back to his side.

I stood up, my back to the window. There was a loud hum from outside. Nussbaum and Greep had succeeded in restarting the engine.

I took a deep sniff. "I wish I had a Hydrogen Hydra to stop that from getting away." The flaming tissues continued to burn as they began to form the ultimate *Gang of Greats* monster, a horrible beast with five heads, enormous wings, fangs and fire-breathing lungs. But the blimp was rising way faster and higher than I'd expected. How was that possible?

"Hydra! Get that blimp!" The Hydra, almost as big as the room now, gave a flap of its wings and swept past me, ripping the remains of the window frame from the walls and knocking me over with the force of the blast.

"Yes!" Cliff yelled. "See. I told you this collection would be valuable someday."

"It won't take too long to replace," I said. I blew my

nose and dropped the tissue onto the floor. I wasn't too careful, and the tissue landed on Algernon's head.

"Thanks for that," he said.

"You're okay!" Cliff yelled again. He picked up the mouse and hugged him. I gave Algernon a high-five. Well, I used my pinky and he used his paw.

The blimp had disappeared into the clouds, pursued by the Hydra. The humming and roaring continued, and then faded away.

"I don't get it. How can the blimp fly so fast with all that reidium inside?"

Algernon jumped onto the windowsill and pointed at the lawn next to Cliff's house. "That reidium?"

We looked down. The entire collection of boxes, bulbs and pencils lay strewn on the grass.

CHAPTER 23

YEP-ILOGUE

Okay, no kidding around this time. This is the real epilogue, you know, with some answers and stuff. So, as far as I know, the Hydra is still chasing the blimp somewhere up in the stratosphere. At least, there haven't been any reports of giant blobs of snot falling from the sky. Or blimps. Although the captain of the other blimp was quoted saying he'd seen a giant five-headed beast fly by his cockpit with, weirdly, a card with a bad drawing of a girl's head on it in its teeth. No one believed him.

Back on solid ground, there was still work to be done. I had made a promise to Miss T. and I delivered on it, if a little late. I conjured up a snot eagle, a pretty big one too, that flew me and Cliff back to Dimly Field.

Cliff was able to join the band for the big worldwide concert, and he tooted up a storm. I even snuck into my seat for the third period. The look on Dad's face when I took his hand and smiled at him . . . Okay, tearing up here. Moving on . . . The Gents won the game 1–0 in triple overtime.

When we got back to Cliff's place, the reidium had vanished. Department C, according to Algernon, was storing it in a safe place to keep it protected. I'm not sure that's the whole story, but it was all Algernon was going to give me. I'd also conjured up a handyman to fix Cliff's house, and that looked better than new.

It might be best to tell you everything else by describing the dinner party we had in my basement the next night. Cliff, Algernon and I ordered some excellent pizza and wings, and even some gourmet Gorgonzola. Algernon patted his stomach and settled into his cushion. "That was delicious," he said.

"Okay, cheese breath," I said. "'Fess up. What happened back there?"

"Yesh," Cliff said, his mouth jammed with pizza.

"Well, as you know, I commandeered the airship to attack Nussbaum's blimp."

"Stowing away is a thing with you," I joked.

"Point taken. I had every intention of shoving the blimp away from Dimly Field and bringing it down by whatever means necessary. Then, when Cliff warned me you were on board, I swerved."

"I was there for that part, genius," I said. "Skip to after that."

"Fine. When the blimps smashed into each other, I jumped ship and held on to the outside rigging. Stupidly, I almost pulled a patch right off, although that did slow the blimp's progress. It also gave me a long bit of rope and an idea. Once we hit Cliff's house, we were steady enough for me to scramble to the propeller. I threw the rope into the blades and they stopped, at least momentarily."

"That's what caused the explosion?"

"No, that was the cheap blaster Greep was using to fire on you. They really do cut corners on the most surprising things."

"Pot, meet kettle," I said. "Does the *C* in Department C stand for cheap?"

"Do you want answers or not?"

"Fine. So back to the reidium?"

"Ah yes. When the rear of the blimp fell to the ground, I jumped inside, sprung the hatch bay, and just let it all tumble out. Then I grabbed one of the loose paint cans and ran alongside the spine of the ship and into the bridge. I believe you know the rest."

"Yeah. We foiled their evil plans."

Algernon smiled and popped another bit of cheese into his mouth. "Indeed we did."

"Any idea why I can read Jess's mind?" Cliff asked, scarfing another chicken wing and licking his fingers.

Disgusting, I thought.

"It's pronounced delicious," Cliff said.

"Proximity . . . possibly," Algernon said. "But that is only a theory. It's quite possible that the collection of tissues in Cliff's room and his, ahem, closeness to you combined to rub some reidium effects off on him."

"Closeness?" Cliff asked.

I quickly changed the subject. "Well, what about the other kids?" I asked. "What's happening with them?"

Algernon stood up and brushed some crumbs off his shirt. "I'm afraid that is not my place to say. Now, if you will excuse me, I must be getting back to my colleagues in the laboratory. We will meet again."

He gave a low bow and waddled away up the basement stairs. We heard RigaTony howl, then the scurrying of tiny feet across the floor. RigaTony gave a sad meow, signalling that Algernon had escaped through a hole in the wall.

"He does like to live on the edge," Cliff joked. "By the way, Fartface, how did the G of G tournament go?"

"It . . ." I stopped. "Wait, what did you call me?" Cliff suddenly looked guilty, his eyes darting around the room. "YOU'RE BEANCOUNTER3000X!"

He hung his head. "Um. Yeah."

"Why are you always trying to kill me?" I howled.

He looked straight at me. "I knew you wanted to get better at the game."

"So you tried to defeat me?"

He shook his head. "No. Well, not really. Think about the past couple of weeks. You need a puffer to walk up the stairs, but when Greep and Nussbaum were trying to kill you, you were able to sprint away on your bike, climb into a garbage truck, and even fight for your life on the bridge of a dumpy blimp."

"What are you saying?"

"I'm saying that you're stronger than you think you are. You always do better when you've got an obstacle in front of you. So I made up an avatar in G of G to, I dunno, push you a bit."

I just stared at him, incredulous.

"It's one of the things I love most about you," he said in a small voice. I snorted, but kept staring. "You've got that puke look on your face again. Are you going to hit me?" He backed away but I leaned right over, and I hugged him, hard. "Can't breathe," he choked.

"Welcome to my life!" I let him go then smiled my best best-friend smile. "Booger-Girl and Toots."

"Inseparable."

CHAPTER 24

EPI-EPILOGUE

Okay, one last detail to pass along, although this isn't about what happened, but about what I think is *going* to happen, if that makes sense. It doesn't really, which is why I'm throwing it in here. I don't even know what it means. Yet.

Anyway, while Cliff and I were sitting there getting all superhero duo-ey, the mail arrived. There is no mail on Sunday in Dimly, which should have triggered something in my brain.

"Jess, a letter," Dad called down from the top of the stairs.

I ran over and he threw it down to me. "Thanks, Dad. Go, Gents!" I said. He smiled, then closed the door before RigaTony could squeeze by.

The envelope was taped together, like it had been opened and resealed about ten times. I turned it over. There was no address or stamp. Just my name written in pencil on a sticker. That sticker was on top of what looked like a dozen other stickers.

"What's that?" Cliff asked.

"Looks like a message about recycling," I said, opening the envelope. Well, it more broke into pieces as I started to tear it open. The letter itself was written on a scrap of what felt like newspaper, in a tiny, tiny script. And it was brief.

Jessica Flem
YOU'RE INVITED!
If you're reading this you survived your mission.
Congratulations!
To celebrate a year of (mostly) successful projects, come to our midsummer potluck picnic for those still alive.
Let us know if you'll bring salad, sandwiches or dessert. (And also cheese.)
Looking forward to seeing whoever is left.

Bernard Cheeper,
Department C Projects Coordination

PS You can bring one guest.

There was an address in Montreal.

I looked at Cliff. *Of course, you're coming too*, I thought.

Cliff smiled. And I smiled too.

And then I blew my nose.

CHAPTER 25

TRIPLE-LOGUE

Sorry to keep throwing these at you, but, oh yeah. Of course Jess won the G of G game.

When I'd gotten home after the game my computer was still on. The word "CONGRATULATIONS" was flashing on the screen.

I looked at my controller, which sat on the couch, covered with a tiny glop of green goo.

That's the end.

Or, is it . . . ?

Yes, actually it is.

Bye.

For now . . .

Acknowledgements

We all have something about ourselves we don't like. I'm old. Look at a recent picture of me. I have a lot of grey hairs. (Heck, I could keel over at any moment!) But here's something I've learned in all these years on this beautiful planet: the stuff you don't like about yourself is still part of who you are. Don't deny it. In fact, it might be the part you come to most identify with as YOU.

Jess's superpower at the end of this book isn't her ability to make snot fighters. Not really. It's that she's come to accept that the part of herself that makes her squirm the most and feel the weirdest is a part of her . . . and can be actually a great part of her.

And, this is also important, Jess's best friend, Cliff, sees this before she does. You will never reach this point of acceptance on your own. Everyone lives with and is surrounded by others. And they will be there to help you along the way. (And you need to help them too.) For me, on this Almost Epic journey, those friends were Ted Staunton and Richard Scrimger. They had an idea for a series of books that would overlap, be funny and fun, and would tell the stories of kids who don't have the "super" superpowers. Their powers would be more . . . almost epic. They asked me if I'd like to join the ride. Saying an emphatic "yes" was possibly the best thing I've done as a writer. Making this book and this series has been a total blast. So a gigantic thanks to them both for reaching out, and for all the great brain-exploding chats about how to tell this story.

I made more friends along the way, all of whom made this book (and me) better in some way. Lesley Livingston is one of the most interesting people you'll ever meet. Just sit down and ask her what she's done for a living and . . . be prepared to be fascinated. And her writing? Wow!!!!! Anne Shone — editor supreme! Her ability to juggle this crazy premise of a book and series was definitely epic. Erin Haggett was there to help herd the various flotsam and jetsam of plot point and character development. Britt Wilson! Such fun images and a great sense of kicking our humble words up a notch. BOOM! The whole gang at Scholastic has been . . . wow. It's an honour to be part of this team. And I can't wait to see what we cook up (or maybe hork up?) next.

But before these people, there was a young boy who blew his nose — a lot. His parents, Blanche and Bernie, loved him and kept him well stocked with snotrags. His brothers, Doug, Mike and Tim, played games with him — and laughed at his nose-blowing. His cousin Dave needs particular thanks. He suffered through a year of sniffling and snurfling and is still (more than) willing to get together over barbequed pizza and some cold beverages.

The boy's grown-up friends don't mention that his nose looks like Rudolph on a bad day. His wife accepts it. His kids, quite frankly, have inherited it. And, he's come to accept that every sunny summer day will come with some pollen and stuffiness. Every cute kitten or puppy will require some level of nostril clearing. And that's totally cool.

So, look . . . things can be really bleak and horrible sometimes. You can feel awkward, gross, weird. And there might be people willing to make you feel that way. But things can also be incredibly awesome. Finding the best way to accept the bad bits with the awesome bits is one of the main tricks of growing up.

KEVIN SYLVESTER is an award-winning writer, illustrator and broadcaster. He writes and illustrates everything from murder mysteries and science fiction to books on sports and financial literacy. His books include the bestselling MiNRS and Neil Flambé series. Kevin's personal superpower is the ability to take a puck off the head and *still* finish a hockey game. He's also known to be able to make a last-second dinner from whatever smells reasonably edible in the fridge. And he can instantly turn circles into cats and ice cream cones into dragons. Well, cat and dragon cartoons anyway.

FOUR BOOKS.
FOUR AUTHORS.
FOUR UNFORGETTABLE
SUPERHEROES.

Mucus Mayhem by Kevin Sylvester
Hey, look, you're holding it in your hand!

What Blows Up by Ted Staunton, available January 2019
Gary "Clumsborg" Lundborg is more than a little surprised to suddenly find himself moving objects with his mind — not gracefully, often distractedly, and only between three and six in the morning. Will this help him become a basketball star? Well, first he must save the world . . .

Super Sketchy by Lesley Livingston, available May 2019
Daisy Kildare is starting over at a new school. Sometimes she wishes she could be anywhere else. But when she uses a certain pencil, Daisy finds she can *turn into* whatever she draws. She just needs to harness that power. If only her drawing skills were a little more accurate . . .

Irresistible by Richard Scrimger, available September 2019
Archie O'Kaye mostly rubs people the wrong way. But when he becomes utterly charming right before everyone's eyes at his thirteenth birthday party, his family and friends know something is up. And they're not the only ones watching . . .

Visit www.scholastic.ca/almost-epic
for chapter excerpts, videos and more!

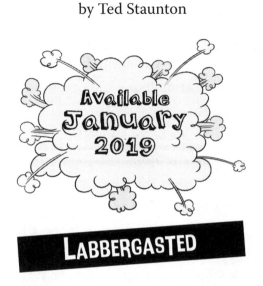

LABBERGASTED

It was past 2:00 a.m. when Gary nodded off. The movie he'd seen earlier had featured a lot of swooping starfighters. Maybe that was why he dreamed the fireplace tongs from the afternoon's testing were sailing around the light fixtures, battling flying tissue boxes.

Noises jerked him awake: shouting, crashes, a thud, then a cascade of *something* falling around him. Gary blinked. Bits of plaster were scattered at his feet. Drops of water pattered on his head. Gary looked up. In front of him one of the light fixtures dangled by a wire. The tongs were rammed into the ceiling, a tissue box impaled on each arm. Tissues wafted like spring snowflakes in Dimly. The sprinkler system had kicked in as well. Amid it all, Dr. Fassbinder was shouting orders to mice in tiny lab coats. *Huh?*

Dr. F. pushed past the light fixture and pumped Gary's hand. His moustache danced wildly. "You did it, Gary! Congratulations!"

Behind Dr. F. mice were swivelling a video camera recording the destruction.

"You did *this*!" cried Dr. F.

"Geez, sorry. I don't—"

"No, it's wonderful! Gary, your powers have kicked in. You must have—" Dr. F. took a deep breath. "Gary, try this. See that chair? Move it." Gary rose. Dr. F. stopped him. "No, with your mind. *Will it* to move."

"You mean, like, um, tele-whatsit?"

"Telekinesis. Exactly. *Imagine* moving it."

Dr. F. didn't seem to be kidding. Gary eyed the chair. It looked heavy. He pushed up his glasses, sucked in a breath, and summoned a big mental push. *Now.* The chair rocketed across the room and bashed into the wall. Mice squeaked and leaped to safety, lab coats billowing like superhero capes.

Gary's mouth opened. "Wow," he finally breathed. "Sorry, I forgot the . . . roller thingies . . ."

"Never mind." Dr. F. reverently patted the dented wall. The mice broke into applause. A tiny voice cried "Bravo!" This was followed by an angry squeak.

Dr. Fassbinder lifted his sneaker from a mouse tail. "Sorry, Elaine. C'mn, everybody. To the lab."

The mice hustled through the door flap. Gary and Dr. Fassbinder followed in the regular way. Behind another door was a room Gary had never seen before: a laboratory, bustling with mice scampering on computer keyboards, lugging test tubes, and wiring connections.

"They're nocturnal," said the doctor, as if that was all that needed explaining.

Other than that, it wasn't much of a lab. The computers were old, the work tables cluttered. There was a microwave, refrigerators labelled *cheese* and *brain samples* and a lounge area with dollhouse furniture. There, two mice putted marbles on a *mini* minigolf course, another stood over a sudoku, chewing a pencil, and one bench-pressed a wrench. In a far corner sat cardboard boxes marked *DIMLY BULB: The Light of Your Life.*

Gary blinked. What was going on? All he'd wanted was a little coordination, maybe some math smarts. "Uh, could I have a glass of water?"

"Sure, there are beakers by the sink. Use your power," said Dr. Fassbinder. "On second thought, let me get it."

The mice took a cheese break, then patched Gary with sensors. Machines beeped and hummed as he guided balloons (tricky), printed on a whiteboard (very tricky), and threw darts (don't ask), using mind power. Then came a couple of accidental don't-asks, involving a tennis racquet and a Bunsen burner. Gary quickly thought the fire extinguisher into action. Unfortunately his glasses had come off. He aimed it at the wrong place and destroyed some computers.

"Not to worry," said Dr. F. "They were old ones."

"Everything in this dump is old," squeaked a voice.

It was all so strange that it was hard to concentrate. After a while Gary's power began fading. By 6:00 a.m. it was gone. He slumped sootily in a tangle of wires. Thirteen years of waiting for three hours of mental *Clumsborg*ing. It hardly seemed fair.

"Don't worry," said Dr. F., nibbling now-smoked cheese. "It's probably a cycle. Your power should return. We'll test again tomorrow night. Now you need some rest. Tell no one. I'll talk to your mom."

"We'll get a budget increase!" cheered a mouse peeling off Gary's sensor stickers.

"Budget, schmudget," groused the voice Gary had heard complaining earlier. "We should be a reality series. That's where the money is. We'd be stars!"

"Claude, this is pure science! Research is its own reward."

The argument was raging when Gary left. In the cab he messaged Jess back in Dimly: "Weirdest visit with dr F evr! We should talkl." Then he fell asleep . . .